Virtual Velocity

Anthony Mora

Black Rose Writing | Texas

This is a work of fiction. Names, characters, businesses, places, events, and incidents are either the products of the author's imagination or used in a fictitious manner. Any resemblance to actual persons, living or dead, or actual events is purely coincidental.

ISBN: 978-1-68433-352-3
PUBLISHED BY BLACK ROSE WRITING
www.blackrosewriting.com

Printed in the United States of America
Suggested Retail Price (SRP) $16.95

Virtual Velocity is printed in Calluna

To Ann, always.

The Trinity: Stella, Pat & Cissy

With special thanks to Rick

Virtual Velocity

Hurricane
Spring 2018

Jake Jensen slipped on his sunglasses and walked out of the Skylight Bookstore into the Los Angeles night. He turned left and headed down Vermont Boulevard. A lanky man in his mid-twenties with deliberately tousled hair and a carefully unshaven face hurried after him.

"That was awesome," he called out, trying to jockey a position next to Jake while maneuvering the broken sidewalk and avoiding those walking up the street. "The Dresden is just a few doors down. Sheila will meet us there."

Jake nodded and continued in silence past Figaro Bistrot and the Thirteenth Church of Christ-Science. He felt his shirtsleeve grabbed and pulled as he reached the Dresden. He turned to see a young, attractive blonde woman hanging on as one would to a dog's leash. "That was great," she gushed excitedly. "That was the best. It was so... I mean it was... it was awesome... we love everything you write, everything you've ever written." She motioned to a petite, moon-faced girl who was trailing her at the word "we." "A picture!" the blonde declared, releasing Jake's shirt and pulling out her iPhone. "That would be great. Amazing. Totally awesome."

Jake stared at her with a somewhat startled expression masked by the dark glasses. He then smiled and nodded.

"Yes!" she cried loudly, while positioning her phone camera. Again she grabbed Jake's shirt and pulled him towards her, positioning him so they were both in the frame. She let go with a loud "Awesome!" as she pushed the camera button on her phone. It was a selfie-plus-one blissathon. "Now, Carly. Hurry," she commanded, motioning her friend into the line of fire.

The blonde turned to the young man standing next to them. "You!" she cried, holding her phone out towards him. "Here, use my phone. Take a picture of the three of us together and then one with just me and Jake and one with just Carly and Jake." She glared at the man until he nodded. She then thrust the phone into his hand.

Taking hold of the phone, the man carefully studied the shot.

"Come on, shoot!" the blonde insisted, wrapping her arm around Jake's waist and pulling him towards her.

The man nodded. "Smile," he said. Taking the assigned photos, he looked somewhat longingly at the blonde, as he handed back her phone. He smiled. Completely ignoring him, she grabbed the phone and dropped it in her purse. Her hand emerged with a felt tip pen. "An autograph. Please," she cried, again grabbing on to Jake's shirt.

"Okay," he said slowly, pronouncing it as two separate words.

"Yes!" she exclaimed. Then, releasing his shirt she hooked her thumbs under her jeans and pulled them down enough to show the top line of her panties. "Don't have any paper. Sign here," she instructed. "Good thing I'm not wearing a thong tonight," she added with a laugh.

"For real," her friend agreed, her grin locked in place.

Jake took the pen and, bending over, carefully wrote "Jake Jensen" on the small strip of fabric.

"Awesome. Now her," the blonde directed, pulling her giggling friend towards Jake. Carly uncomfortably shuffled towards him. After a slight pause, she pulled up her blouse enough to reveal her bra. "I don't wear... you know," she explained.

Jake nodded, frowned, and dutifully signed her bra.

"Awesome!" the blonde exclaimed. She leaned towards Jake and kissed his cheek. "You're the absolute best," she yelled. The two then turned and, locking arms, ran up the street back towards the Skylight Bookstore.

Jake and the tall somewhat ruffled young man silently stood and watched until the girls disappeared into the bookstore.

"I didn't think that happened to authors," the younger man said as he and Jake opened the door and entered the Dresden.

"I take umbrage at that," Jake growled as he scanned the room.

"I didn't mean it wasn't justified," the young man replied hurriedly. "I don't mean that you don't deserve that. Your work truly is amazing. I mean it's..."

"Relax," Jake said. "You're right. As far as I know, that doesn't happen to writers and it never happened to me," he paused thoughtfully and added, "until a few years ago. So," he continued as he looked around the bar, "where did Sheila say she'd be?" He stared at the young man. "It's John, right?"

John smiled and nodded. "I'll check," he said, walking from the bar into the white tabled adjacent restaurant. The Dresden was empty that night. Two couples sat in the restaurant. The bar, which overflowed during the weekend, was relatively quiet. "Not here yet, I guess," he said as he returned.

Jake removed his sunglasses, carefully slid them into his pocket, and again scanned the room. "She's never not been at one of my readings and she's never late. I'm always late." He paused and again looked around the room. Four people sat at the bar. The tables were empty. The small stage sat silent. "Let's stay in the bar for now," he continued, as he walked over to an empty table. "We'll see her as she enters." Sitting, he motioned for John to do the same. He then waved to a waitress and ordered two beers.

John nervously checked his watch and continued to scan the

room. "She said she'd meet us here after the reading. Said I was to wait until she was here to start the interview."

"You're here. I'm here. Start the interview," Jake directed.

"She gave specific instructions," John explained. "I gave her my word."

"I respect that," Jake said. "A man of his word. Now start the interview."

John pulled out his phone. "I'll just text her. I'm sure she'll get right back. She's always on top of things." He paused and then added, "I want to let you know how excited I am that you're giving your first interview in five years to me. Your books are incredible, amazing." John paused, thinking he was going overboard, not acting sufficiently journalistic. He then added, "This will be my first cover story."

"You ask Sheila out yet?" Jake asked.

John shook his head as though denying an accusation. "I'm just here to do the interview."

Jake shrugged. "So, what is this place?" he asked, looking around the bar. "A Vonnegut homage?"

John stared, a confused look on his face.

"This place... the Dresden. Vonnegut... *Slaughterhouse-Five*..." Jake sighed. "Nothing. Forget it."

"Oh, yeah. Right," John replied, his facial expression registering embarrassment. "Vonnegut. Right. I don't really know the area. I Googled Los Feliz," he continued. "This place was close to the bookstore." Looking down, he pushed the answer button on his phone. "Sheila!" he cried, placing the phone to his ear. "Are you close? Jake said he'd like to start the interview now." John looked up. "It's okay if I call you Jake, right?"

Jake shrugged.

"Mr. Jensen is ready to start the interview," John announced formally. "I know I promised not to begin before you arrived, but he's getting a bit impatient and I think…"

"Impatient, irritable, and bordering on violent," Jake added. He looked up and smiled broadly as the waitress placed down their beers.

"Yes. Sure. Of course," John said, holding the phone close to his mouth, his voice wavering as though he was running a race. "I completely understand. We'll wait until you get here." Disconnecting the call, he looked at Jake. "She doesn't want me to start until she's here. She was quite adamant."

"She's good at adamant," Jake replied. "Maybe you can take her out after the interview. Women can be interesting when they're adamant. I, in turn, will go home to my cat and my pug and have a relaxing evening reading a book that bores the hell out of me."

John smiled.

"The pug snores even when she's awake," Jake continued. "For now, I call her 'Cat.' The cat loves the pug but is too dim to realize she thinks she's an imbecile. Cat's current name is 'Dog.' They don't like the novel I'm reading either."

"Why read it?" John asked.

"How will I know if I hate it unless I read it?" Jake paused. "Besides, readers are a dying breed. Novels began losing steam in the 20th century, they're now barely limping along. Gasping. Will be gone soon."

"But you… you still sell books," John said, as though proving a point. "You still have a huge audience."

"Artificially created and dying off one by one. There is no technician left to refill the candy machine. When they're gone— they're gone. I used to think it strange that most people had no idea who Thomas Wolf was. Now you get that same glassy-eyed stare when you mention Tom Wolf. Novelists are anachronisms, even the spanking new writers." Jake sighed dramatically. "Well this is getting maudlin. Go ahead, start the interview."

The two looked up as the bartender marched towards them. "One of you named John?" he asked gruffly.

John nodded.

"There's a call for you," he said, nudging his head towards the phone, making it clear this was not accepted policy.

John shot a confused look at Jake. He then quickly stood and followed the bartender to the phone.

Jake sat back, pulled his pen out of his shirt pocket and carefully placed it on the table. He watched John animatedly talking on the phone, as he took a drink.

"It was Sheila," John said, breathlessly running back to the table. "She's in a bit of a mess. Her phone was lost or stolen. She said all her numbers are in her phone and she doesn't know any by heart, which is why she called the restaurant. I told her we were going to be here," he added as way of explanation. "That's the trouble with technology, don't you think? Nobody remembers anyone's phone numbers anymore. It's an outsourced memory which can too easily be lost." John paused, waiting for a reaction from Jake to his profound observation. When there was none, he continued. "Anyway, she knew we were here, so she called the Dresden. She said she'd be here soon and I should wait to do the interview until she arrives. She's in West Hollywood."

"West Hollywood to Los Feliz on a Saturday night will take the better part of a week." Jake paused and groaned aloud theatrically. "Doesn't trust me. Afraid I'll go rogue. But that's what you're praying for."

"I just want to write the best article. I…"

"Maybe if I drink enough, without Sheila here to police the

situation, just maybe I'll totally derail, go completely off the track, crash, burn and explode right in front of you." Jake stared at John with a "you know I'm right" grin and nodded.

"That's not what I want," John said defensively. "I want an honest, authentic..."

"You want a fucking train wreck," Jake pronounced.

John shook his head. "You used to be a journalist. That's not what *you* wanted."

"Sure it was," Jake said. "Besides, I was a rock journalist. There's an oxymoron. Who the fuck cares what rock stars think about anything?"

"A lot of people do," John replied.

"Idiots," Jake said with a shrug, not clarifying whether he was referring to the rock stars or the public. "I used to like your job," he added, "interviewing people. I liked tossing out the questions and then kicking back and pretending I was interested, letting people ramble on and on. I'd tune out and get paid for it. That was nice. A smile and nod at the appropriate time. A well-placed 'interesting,' or 'really.' Sometimes I listened to their records, but never gave a shit about what they had to say. Now I don't even listen to their music."

"Never?" John asked.

Jake shook his head.

"But when you think of all the people you interviewed, Bowie, Jagger, Prince, Petty..."

"I *don't* think about them." Jake looked away, a bored expression on his face.

"Sorry," John replied. "I'm just trying to..."

"We might as well eat something, right?" Jake said, motioning again to the waitress. "We need to send down some reinforcements." The waitress arrived and Jake, without consulting John, ordered appetizers. "So," Jake said, "until Sheila gets here, apart from anything to do with my writing, or anything you can write about, or publish, what would you like to talk about?"

"You really didn't know who Virtual Velocity was?" John asked, "I mean before that Coachella concert."

"It's the title of one of my novels," Jake replied, a tinge of wariness in his voice.

"I know," John replied. "But the band… you'd really never heard of the band?"

Jake shook his head. "I had no idea who they were or that they had appropriated my book's name. Didn't much care when I learned about it. And, anticipating a question that will surface soon, according to Webster's, virtual velocity is 'a minute hypothetical displacement, assumed in analysis to facilitate the investigation of statical problems. With respect to any given force of a number of forces holding a material system in equilibrium, it is the projection, upon the direction of the force, of a line joining its point of application with a new position of that point indefinitely near to the first, to which the point is conceived to have been moved, without disturbing the equilibrium of the system, or the connections of its parts with each other. Strictly speaking, it is not a velocity but a length.'" Jake paused and took a drink. "I memorized that after having to answer that question countless times. That has nothing to do with why I named my book *Virtual Velocity*, but it is a definition of virtual velocity."

John nodded as though mulling over Jake's response. "I saw that clip of you on stage with the band in Coachella," he said. "That was awesome."

Jake grimaced, reacting to the sound of the last word. "Terrifying," he corrected. "Like being picked up by a hurricane and dropped in another world. Wizard of Oz time. But that was a tornado." Jake paused and took a drink.

"Speaking of hurricanes," he continued, leaning closer to John and staring intensely, "do you know that a hurricane swooped up a swarm of locusts in Africa and carried them hundreds, maybe thousands of miles to somewhere in the Caribbean? And they survived the trip. Well a lot of them did. So, this place where the hurricane dropped them had never experienced locusts, and suddenly there's a voracious swarm dropped from the sky by a hurricane, cutting a swath through the land and devouring everything in its path. Amazing, when you think of it." He leaned back and looked towards the door. "So, think of me as the locust. Virtual Velocity, the band, not my book, created the hurricane and Sheila directed it to swoop me up and there I flew. The metaphor falls apart when it comes to the locusts being dropped and devouring everything in their path... but I'm working on it."

"It helped bring you to a whole new audience. It..."

"You say that as though there was an old audience," Jake corrected. "I had, what? Maybe a hundred loyal readers. After Coachella I became the Beanie Baby, or the Pet Rock or whatever, the flavor-of-the-month. Suddenly I was seen as visible, cool, trending, hurricane-propelled. My books actually began to sell." Jake paused as the waitress brought the appetizers. He picked one up, ate it, offered one to John, and then continued. "I started making money as a writer. A novelist who doesn't write fantasy, horror, or science fiction that makes money; how's that for an oxymoron? That's our second oxymoron. Then came the parties, red carpet events, dinners, speaking engagements, interviews, and media appearances. The hurricane dragged me along rag doll-like. Went for the ride longer than I should have. Stayed on it for two years. Had to get out of its path before I was annihilated." Jake paused and stared at John with a bored expression. He then looked towards the bar.

John followed his gaze. A senior hipster couple, a lone man of indeterminate age wearing a black beret and a woman looking to be in her early thirties with a died black page-boy sat at the bar. The woman seemed to be whispering to the bartender. They leaned into each other as though sharing stolen secrets. She was dressed in a long, tight, bare-shouldered electric-blue dress. Tattoos snaked up her right arm like a multicolored long glove. The couple was talking together animatedly. The lone man silently drank. "Weird, isn't it?" John asked as he stared at them. "They don't know we're here doing this interview. It's as though we're in the 1920s and I'm interviewing Hemingway or Fitzgerald and everyone in the bar is completely oblivious to the whole thing."

"You do drugs?" Jake asked.

"I'm serious. The comparison is exact." He paused and then asked, "So, you just disappeared?"

Jake stretched and ran his hands through his hair. "It's almost impossible to disappear now. There are legions of online stalkers who do spy work for one another. Until Spain. It was quiet there. The hurricane and insanity lulled to a low roar. Actively disappearing takes effort but is a wonderful way to live. I recommend it."

"But you're back. You're here. I'm here interviewing you."

"Contractual," Jake said, almost apologetically. He picked up his pen and leaned over as though about to write on a napkin. He then paused and carefully placed it back down. "My new novel is being released and it's the fifteenth anniversary of *Virtual Velocity*. Unbeknownst to me, I signed a contract which obliges me to help market my books. It mentions interviews and bookstore appearances, but," he added with a deep grin, "they screwed up by not mentioning how many. There's no number. So, by doing tonight's book reading and this interview, I've basically fulfilled my contractual obligations. It's my official swan song." Jake paused thoughtfully. "Can locusts sing swan songs?"

"I'm doing the final Jake Jensen interview?" John said, speaking primarily to himself. "How fucking cool is that?"

Jake looked away.

"But that can't be it," John said. "Sheila has you booked for the 2020 Coachella. She told me all about it. It sounds amazing." John paused and grimaced. "Shit," he snapped, "I probably wasn't supposed to tell you. She was maybe keeping it as a surprise. I didn't mean to... don't tell her that..."

"Makes no difference," Jake said, with a magician-like wave of his hand. "I won't be there."

"But Sheila..."

"Will rise to the occasion."

John nodded. "So after this interview—you're going to disappear again?"

"I'll walk away. Through there," Jake said, looking up and motioning towards the door. "Won't be missed. Sheila's shepherding others through the hurricane now. She enjoys sending people streaking through the sky. Think she's been offered her own reality show. She'll be the one riding the storm. Maybe that was always the plan."

John stared at Jake with a thoughtful frown. "I still don't understand how you ended up at Coachella."

Jake sat back and stretched. "Until Sheila gets here, none of this is on the record. Doctor's orders."

John nodded.

Jake nodded in return. "I was at home brooding when I got a call from some guy saying that Vinyl would love to meet me and would like for me to go on stage with the band at Coachella so that he could introduce me to the audience. I didn't have a clue what he was talking about. I had stopped doing the rock writing bit years before and no longer knew or cared anything about that world. The only 'vinyl' I knew was a spinning disk. I was about to hang up, when he added that all my expenses would be paid and that they'd pay me ten thousand dollars for my time and the inconvenience." Jake laughed. "That was when? 2010? I had been broke before the recession, but then I was really broke. I was sitting on a metal folding chair next to a card table that served as my dining room table, trying to figure out how I'd pay that month's rent and this guy's offering ten grand for me to go to a concert. I said if they could wire me the money immediately, I was on board. They did and I was."

"You really didn't know that the band was named after your novel?"

Jake paused, sat back, and folded his arms. "When doing an interview, don't ask the same question more than once."

John nodded, noticeably cringing. "But I can't believe that you really didn't... I mean those guys are huge, awesome..." John paused and then sheepishly added, "Sorry."

"They used my title. It happens," Jake said, picking up his pen and pointing it at John as he spoke. "Happened to Burroughs all the time. The term 'heavy metal' first appeared in print in *The Soft Machine*. One of the characters is described as 'the Heavy Metal Kid.' There was also a band called Soft Machine. I saw them open for Hendrix. The drummer was also the lead singer and wore only a jockstrap, if I recall. Anyway, I think Burroughs again used heavy metal in *Nova Express* or *Wild Boys*. Or something. Don't remember." Jake took a drink and checked to see his sunglasses were in place. "The Doors," he continued, "and Steppenwolf. Dime a dozen."

"Can I use this stuff?" John asked, opening his notebook and pulling out his pen. "I mean this is about rock and literature and not about you, so it's not off the record, right? I mean, it's useable material, right?"

Jake shrugged noncommittally. "Steely Dan took their name from a steam-powered dildo that appears in *Naked Lunch*. Duran Duran based the song 'Wild Boys' on Burroughs' novel. And, leaving the Burroughs, The Velvet Underground named themselves after Michael Leigh's early 1960's book of the same name. I think it was described somewhere as being about 'aberrant sexual behavior between consenting adults,' the novel that is."

"And Modest Mouse, right?" John added, hoping to impress Jake who simply stared at him. "Their name," John continued, his smile fading, "it comes from a Virginia Woolf story. Right?" he added after a pause.

Jake took a drink, wrote on his napkin and then looked up. "I think Burroughs holds the record." He paused and looked towards the bar. "Interviewed him once, he was..."

"You interviewed William Burroughs?"

Jake stared at him. "Didn't I just say that I..."

"Yeah, but, Burroughs. How cool. What was he...?" John stopped his fan-boy questioning mid-sentence. He shook his head and took a drink. "Sorry."

After a brief pause, Jake began. "I think I lied and said I had an assignment, which I didn't, but his rep bought it and set it up. It was a Saturday morning at an elegantly furnished home in Brentwood. Must have been the home of a rich patron. I always wanted one of those. Do they still dole out patrons?" Jake stared at John as if awaiting an answer.

John shrugged uncomfortably.

"I forget the name of the poet who was there with him," Jake continued, "a rotund, smiling guy. He answered the door, ushered me in, directed me into a large living room with ornate furniture and a baby grand. Waved his hand like a maître d' inviting me in. He directed me to sit on a very plush couch."

"'Mr. Burroughs will be in shortly,' the guy announced."

"I'm sure he said, *Mr. Burroughs* for effect. Seriously doubt he referred to him as Mr. Burroughs at any other time."

"The guy then cheerfully asked, 'Would you care for water, coffee, wine?'"

"I shook my head and thanked him."

"'Very well,' he replied."

"He then bowed, walked out into the backyard and spent the rest of the time I was there splashing in a large swimming pool filled with unnaturally blue water. As the poet splashed, I sat and waited in the living room, wishing I had made notes or prepared. But that wasn't my style.

"Then Burroughs entered, tall, gaunt, and unsmiling, wearing his trademark suit and hat. He sat and stared. We stared a lot as I recall. I began by asking about the cut-up technique. His clipped response was that he was no longer interested in the cut-up technique. So we stared some more." Jake paused, took a drink and looked around the bar.

"I'm sure she'll be here soon," John said. "Probably parking now."

Jake nodded and continued. "My next few follow-up questions all elicited a similar response. His answers were clipped, monosyllabic, abrupt, and without any change in expression. I considered leaving. And then something shifted. He smiled, leaned back, and began to talk to me. For some reason I chose to ask if he believed in God. His answer was immediate and definitive. 'Many and always at war.' He believed time travel was not only possible, but happening, explained how Ginsberg had been the PR genius behind the myth and legend of the Beats, how the information that the government released on heroin and addiction was laughable and totally wrong and that heroin addiction was a disease of exposure. He believed that power addiction was the worst kind." Jake paused and frowned, as if trying to recall. "I asked him something about the history of the Beats. Some kind of innocuous question. He stopped me mid-sentence and pronounced 'All history is fiction!'" Jake laughed and took a drink. "I didn't get it back then. I totally missed it. I thought it was Burroughs trying to sound cool, or come up with a good sound bite that I could pull from the interview." He looked at John, his eyes narrowing. "That is what's stayed with me the most. It is. It's all fiction. Stories. There are no nonfiction writers. Some know it, others don't have a clue. They believe it. History is the adult Santa Claus. One thing you can say for novelists, and, believe me, you can't say much, is that we admit it. We write fiction. It's made up. It's all bullshit."

John nodded as he rapidly wrote. "Not using any of this," he explained as he looked up, "just notes for me. Unless you say it's okay... once Sheila gets here. So that was it? With Burroughs?"

Jake shrugged. "He liked living in New York. Said it was like living in a village. He walked wherever he wanted to go and his version of Manhattan consisted of only a few blocks.

"As the conversation continued, Burroughs, although never becoming animated, loosened up. He smiled. Laughed. At the end of the interview, he walked me to the door and as I left, he said, 'Come to New York, stop by; I'll make you breakfast and we can continue talking.' I liked the memory I was left with of Burroughs in his trademark suit and an image of a future where the author of *Naked Lunch* would cook me breakfast." Jake paused and took a drink. "He moved to Lawrence, Kansas. They've dedicated a creek, a nature trail, and even a playground to him. A children's playground dedicated to William Burroughs. What could be more appropriate?"

"Burroughs. That is so fucking cool," John said. Putting down his pen, he paused and looked up. "But I still don't get how you ended up on stage with Virtual Velocity."

"We're again entering off-the-record terrain."

John nodded and closed his notebook.

"Place your pen next to mine," Jake instructed, placing his pen down. "It's like putting both our guns on the table."

John did as instructed. "I watched the video of that concert," he said. "It was awesome…"

"Please do not say that word again," Jake commanded.

John flinched and nodded.

Jake nodded in return and continued. "They sent a car for me, a shiny stretch limo I might add—then a first for me. I met Vinyl and we talked for a bit. Nice guy. Very gracious. Had actually read my novels. I was then taken to my hotel. We were somewhere in the desert. Don't know where, but the room was very plush, at least by Jake Jensen standards of the time. And then a few hours later some guy picked me up and drove me to the concert. It's very tribal out there. Woodstock, without any message or point of view, in the desert. So this guy snaked me through security backstage. That wasn't that new for me. I'd covered quite a few bands from backstage during my journalism years. But this was different. I wasn't writing, not on assignment, not on the clock, no responsibility. No pretending to be interested or impressed. Plus, I'd lost track of the rock world by then. Things had changed."

"What had changed?" John asked.

Jake stared at him as though considering his question. He shrugged and then continued. "It. Me."

"But Coachella is cool, right?"

"Cool? Take a basically uninhabited desert, then fill it with people—move the city to a deserted space and pretend you're not right where you started. Seemed a bit pointless. Regardless, this guy delivers me to the dressing room and Vinyl runs over and hugs me like we're old friends. Does some introductions, some quick-talking and glad-handing with who knows whom and then the band gets the word they're on. Out they march and my driver grabs me by the arm and delivers me to the edge of the stage."

"Backstage at Coachella at a Virtual Velocity concert," John said. "That is so fucking aweso... cool."

Jake shrugged. "I was backstage with the Stones, Neil Young, Petty, Prince..."

"Yeah," John said somewhat dismissively, "but still, this was Coachella, Virtual Velocity... Muse was there, right?"

Jake simply stared.

"Yeah," John continued with a nod, answering his own question. "Muse, Pavement, Faith No More and Echo & the Bunnymen and MGMT and..."

"Sly & the Family Stone. That was maybe the only band I knew. They'd aged." He paused thoughtfully. "Echo & the Bunnymen—I remember them." He stopped, took a drink and checked his watch. "So, I'm back there watching the concert and then there's a break; Vinyl quiets the crowd and announces that he'd like to bring out some friends. The crowd erupts as a parade of rock stars start marching in. They must have been on the other side of the stage, because I hadn't seen any of them. A strange assortment. Rockers from different generations start marching on stage, Ray Davies, Trent Reznor, Avril Lavigne, Elvis Costello, Billy Corgan... some others I didn't know, but the crowd seemed to. Everyone was going crazy. Vinyl raised his hand to somewhat silence the crowd. He turned towards me, pointed theatrically, and a spotlight, a blindingly-bright spotlight, hit me. It was like a pinpoint attack. Vinyl then declared: 'And now I want to bring out the guy who named the band. America's greatest living writer...' He kept talking but I basically went blank. I remember someone behind me shoving me onto the stage and then I was hypnotically walking towards Vinyl while thousands of people who had no idea who I was, and only cared because Vinyl told them to, howled and screamed their heads off. Vinyl draped his arm around me and again introduced me. He bent down, picked up a copy of *Virtual Velocity*, and waved it above himself like a flag. It was apparently on all of those huge video screens they now have at concerts. He then turned to his band, counted down from four and they broke into a cover of 'Lola' by the Kinks. Vinyl draped his arm around me again, pulled me towards the mic, and there I was looking like a shell-shocked idiot and singing *Lola, la, la, la, la Lola* with everyone on stage. It felt like, I suppose, standing in front of a jet during takeoff feels. The next thing I remember is being back in the dressing room, frozen, immobile, in shock."

"Amazing. I can use this, right?" John asked. Without pausing he continued. "And Sheila, she was there. That's where you met, right? That's where it all started."

"Sheila was there doing an article or profile on Vinyl, or the band. She came up to me, introduced herself and said that I should have my PR rep post the concert footage ASAP. She was dressed for battle—short skirt, tight blouse, lethal heels. But I was nearly catatonic and I replied with a blank stare. She waited for a few seconds and seeing I was unresponsive, continued, explaining that the video could go viral. At that point, I thought of viral as having to do with infection—something to avoid at all cost. 'Call your PR person and tell her to jump on it!' she all but demanded."

"'I don't have one,' I said, somewhat embarrassed by the

admission, 'the publisher does the PR for my books.'"

"She stared at me with that incredulous look you've probably seen. 'Yeah?' she replied a bit too caustically for my liking, 'and how is that working out?'"

"I was a bit taken aback by the question. As I was considering my response, she grabbed my arm and pulled me towards a corner of the room."

"'You really don't have anyone representing you?' she asked in a loud whisper, her eyes narrowing as she spoke."

"I nodded, assured by her tone that I had made a dreadful mistake. 'But you're a published writer,' she pronounced. 'A famous writer.'"

"'A barely-published little-known and less-read writer,' I corrected."

"'Not after tonight!' she exclaimed. 'At least not if you work it right. This!' she said, with a sweep of her arm. 'What happened here. Tonight. It can take you to a whole different level, get you on the radar of people who never knew you existed. This could be life changing. But you have to jump on it—now! You will never get this chance again.'"

"She paused and, staring at me with a defiant expression, announced, 'I can make it happen.'"

"'You want me to hire you?' I asked, thinking that this was a rather over-the-top pitch for a job."

"She shook her head. 'Once it works you can pay me whatever you think is fair.'"

"'Why?' I asked."

"'Because I can do it. Look,' she said, increasing the pressure on my arm as she spoke, 'this will brand me as well as you. Once I pull this off, make you a star, there will be a line waiting to hire me.'"

"'I thought you were a journalist,' I said."

"'Yeah, but I like to be able to pay my bills. I'm starting a media company, building a media empire.'"

"'And I'm your first client?'"

"She paused. Her eyes again narrowed. 'Exactly,' she said with a laugh. 'Look, this can change both of our lives. If it doesn't work, there's no charge. But it will. What do you have to lose?'"

"'Sleep,' I said with a half-hearted attempt at humor. She raised an eyebrow and stared at me."

"I shrugged and asked, 'How do we start?'"

"As though the power had been switched on, her eyes gleamed. 'Prepare for lift off!' she declared, wrapping me in a hug. 'This is going to be fucking awesome—yes, she said "awesome"—but,' she added, her smile fading, 'I need you to work with me. I'm going to take you out of your comfort zone. You need to trust me, do what I tell you, jump on this rocket and take the ride.' She took a step back and held out her hand to secure the deal. I remember staring down at it for a few seconds, wondering exactly what I was agreeing to. I then clasped her hand in mine and shook it."

"'Deal?' she asked, her eyes locked on mine."

"'Deal,' I replied."

"'Yes!' she cried aloud, raising up her arm palm open in high-five invitation. I accepted, slapping my palm against hers. 'Yes,' she repeated. 'We'll review things in a month. I just need you to work with me, do what I tell you and I'll make you the most famous writer on the planet.'"

"I must have grimaced."

"She then did that thing where her eyes laser in on you. She countered with, 'I'm going to make you the most famous *literary* writer on the planet.'"

"I laughed, surprised by her response. Surprised, she threw

'literary' in to sweeten the deal. 'Deal,' I repeated."

Jake paused, took a drink, and sat back. "That launched a perfect storm. As she predicted, the concert footage went viral. Via her magic, I leapfrogged from an unknown novelist who writes books that are read on a few college campuses, to a mass-marketed product. She turned 'literary' from the financial kiss of death into a branding cash cow. Transformed my normally dead-end literary bona fides into a cool, hip merchandising venture. The video kept gaining traction. I was the elephant in the room, or in this case, on the stage. The weird unknown, uncomfortable nobody singing with rock royalty. Sheila used the who-doesn't-belong-in-this-picture approach, and it worked. I wasn't just a novelty; I was a culturally hip uber-cool novelty. Suddenly my books were read, well, at least bought, not because of my writing, but because of Vinyl's directive and footage slinging round the globe of me with the rock gods. Their fame was infectious. Sheila's spin was that the band was my creation; there would have been no Virtual Velocity without me—an updated incarnation of Warhol and the Velvet Underground—how much cooler can you be than that?" Jake paused, as though awaiting an answer.

John stared, a pensive almost solemn expression on his face, and silently nodded.

Jake laughed and continued. "I went from doing readings in half-filled library auditoriums with folding chairs, to doing those New York Times discussions and having people actually pay to hear me blather on. Then a full speaking tour launched, but not a regular tour. Sheila figured out a way to have the likes of Sia and Eminem drop in. I'd read and then they would do some spoken word bit. She turned the readings into live social media-driven pop-up art events. Celebrities selfishly jumped on board.

"My book, which had previously sold a few hundred copies, was soon going into its fifth printing and making its way to the big screen. I went on for the ride but had no clue where it was taking me. After the film version of *Virtual Velocity* was in pre-production, the Hollywood flood-gates opened. Films and TV pilots were thrown at me like red meat. The stuff I was given was all very heady, dark, depressing—what the film world thinks of as serious art. Somehow Hollywood's conception of 'literary' means dank, ironic, cruel. Think the pornography of despair—they love that." Jake paused and took a drink. "Between you and me, that shit bores the hell out of me as much as staring glassy-eyed at Facebook does." Jake picked up his pen and began to draw on a napkin. "Doodling relaxes me," he explained, looking up at John. "Funny how easy it all was this time, how it all just happened, just cascaded in." He paused and smiled. "When it first came out, I tried to get *Virtual Velocity* made as a film. Didn't have a fucking clue."

"Didn't work, eh?" John asked.

"A disaster. A psychopath latched on to me—or me to her." He looked up quizzically. "I've never figured that one out. Took a ride on an avalanche. And as we hurled down, she spit out names like a machine gun. Not only spit 'em out, she actually knew them and not only knew them, introduced me, brought them to the table. Well, some of them. But it didn't matter. They say it's who you know in this city. Bullshit. She knew everybody. Didn't make a fucking bit of difference. It's all about how the stars align. That," Jake said decisively, "is what it all comes down to." He then returned to doodling.

"Interesting," John said with a nod. "You're into astrology."

Jake paused, looked up, glared at John. "I'm into astrology?" he repeated slowly. "You didn't just say that, did you?"

"No, kidding," John said with a shake of his head. "A joke, just kidding, being sarcastic. We were talking about how the film got made this time around, about the other offers that came your way," he said in an effort to get the interview back on track.

"Never had so much money thrown my way to write—God knows what. They paid, so I wrote."

"That's cool," John said, hearing Jake's full backstory for the first time.

Jake shrugged and laid his pen down next to John's. "Trouble was those gigs involved working with other writers, with showrunners, with—people! Novelists generally bitch about the fact that it's such a lonely, solitary profession, but that's what I always loved about it. That's what I crave. And all that was taken from me. Work, which used to mean me, a cup of coffee, a desk, a laptop, and Cat and Dog, suddenly erupted into writers' meetings, lunches, interviews, photo shoots, parties, and TV writing assignments designed to create fiction by committee. All that horrified me. I was used to not only writing alone, but being left alone, invisible, unnoticed. That was gone. My life was gone." He paused thoughtfully. "So I left. It's not so easy playing Walden now. But I'm slowly disappearing, evaporating, becoming happily invisible again."

"But you're back," John declared. "With tonight's reading and this interview, you're back on the radar. This is your comeback."

Jake shook his head. "Like I told you, I'm back contractually. I'm here because I have to be. Then I disappear." He put his fingers together and opened them. "Poof."

"But this article is just the first. She told me that..." John paused. "Does Sheila know?"

John shrugged. He then took a drink. "She probably has an inkling. It's worked for Sheila. She's now the dreamland kingmaker on steroids. Every writer, filmmaker and musician is standing in line, begging her to do her magic for them. She's the hurricane creator, the miracle girl." Jake looked at his watch and raised an eyebrow. "And she's nowhere to be found." He paused and then started to stand. "Maybe you can email me some questions down the line."

"But—you can't just go," John said as he anxiously checked his phone.

"Chances are, I can." Jake replied.

John began to write a hurried text. "We promised Sheila we'd be here. Maybe we could just start the interview and..."

"Anything we talk about sans Sheila is off the record. None of this is of any use to you—or me. Let's cut our losses."

"A few more minutes," John pleaded, resisting his impulse to reach out and grab Jake's arm. "She'll be here any second. I'm sure. Five minutes."

Jake sighed melodramatically, sat back and took a drink. He looked at John and asked, "You ever go to POP?"

"Pop?" John repeated.

"P-O-P, Pee-Oh-Pee, Pacific Ocean Park. An amusement park in Santa Monica. It closed in 1967."

"I wasn't even born then."

"Depressed the hell out of me when it closed," Jake said.

"I think I've heard of it. You went there a lot?" John asked, grabbing on to a conversational lifeline.

"Nautical-themed amusement park at Pier Avenue," Jake said, slowly peeling off the label on his beer. "Don't remember if it was technically Santa Monica or Venice. Was on a pier. Supposed to give Disneyland a run for its money. Didn't do much of anything, but when it left, a bit of L.A. slid into the ocean. It signaled what was to follow. L.A. is fading," Jake pronounced, "receding, diminishing as we sit here. We are fading."

John dutifully nodded.

"A city vanishing," Jake said, leaning towards John as though sharing a deep secret. "In Silverlake there was Netty's, the Backdoor Bakery, and Hard Times. In Santa Monica there was The Broken Drum and Zucky's on Wilshire and the Olympic Drive-in on Bundy and Olympic. A drive-in right smack in Santa Monica. Technically it was west L.A., but still..." Jake paused and laughed. "You ever go to Zucky's?"

John shook his head.

Jake looked towards the door. "Is five minutes up yet?"

"What was Pacific Ocean Park like?" John replied, also glancing at the door.

Jake paused. He grinned. "It stretched out over the water. It was small. You could walk around it in ten minutes as I remember. It seemed to already be on its last leg when it opened. But you had the ocean, the rides, and barkers. Its seediness gave it a mystical carnival feel, out of a Ray Bradbury novel. There was one of those rides that turns faster and faster and then the bottom falls and centrifugal force keeps you stuck against the wall." Jake picked up his pen and twirled his hand around, spinning it faster and faster. He smiled and placed it back on the table. "Took that ride every time I went. So this one time, my friend and I get on and it starts spinning and the bottom gives way and it keeps spinning faster and it just keeps spinning. We were on it for a while. A long while. And it just kept going 'round and 'round and I'm whipsawing my head as we spin, trying to find the guy who works the ride. But he's nowhere to be found. He's gone. Then I catch a glimpse of him mid-turn, then another and once every revolution there he is and he's not anywhere near the ride. He's in this kind of alleyway with this blonde girl in this multi-colored flowered dress and she seems to be a midget. After a few rotations, I figure out she's no midget. This damn girl is on her knees and is going down on him. He's gone, completely forgotten about us. And we keep spinning and now that I know the ship has been deserted, I start freaking out. By that time, all of us on the ride are yelling our heads off. And everyone passing by just figures we're having one hell of a good time." Jake paused, shook his head and laughed. "It went on for a while. I remember the music playing over the loudspeaker. It was 1965 or ´66, we spun out of control to 'Summer in the City,' 'Wild Thing,' 'Devil with a Blue Dress,' 'Good Lovin´.' Jake paused. "You know those songs?"

"I think so," John replied tentatively. He didn't.

Jake's left eyebrow snaked up. "Any of them?"

"Maybe 'Wild Thing,'" John lied.

Jake stared at him doubtfully. "Anyway, the flowered dress that girl was wearing is what I focused on. That became my touchstone, my frame of reference. I'd wait to see that dress during each revolution. Every turn I tried to remember a different color, or fold, or petal. It kept me sane. Then finally, after what seemed like hours of spinning the jerk comes back and lets us off. I wanted to punch him, but I could barely walk as I stumbled off the ride. That gave me PTSD, you know. I ended up with a bad case of claustrophobia for years."

"But you were outside."

"Outside, but locked in a small space," Jake explained, staring at John intensely and leaning back. "Triggered years of claustrophobia. Anyway, I saw that flowered dress again, years later. That changed my life," he added as a throwaway. Jake paused, took a drink, and stared at the door. He then turned towards John. "I think we have been stood up, my friend. What do you say, we cut our losses?"

"She'll be here any second," John assured. "How did it change your life?"

Jake laughed. "Paddling upstream, aren't you? You're earning whatever they're paying you tonight."

John soldiered on. "Did you ever write the story of the girl in the colored dress?"

Jake picked up his pen and held it as though it was a dart he was about to throw.

"You said it was life-changing," John continued.

Jake placed the pen down and stared at John. "I write fiction."

An uncomfortable silence followed.

"Memoirs have become an important genre," John said somewhat hesitantly. "Some of the biggest selling…"

"I told you. All fiction. When writers don't have anything to write about, they write memoirs."

"But you have to admit there are some pretty impressive memoirs…"

"When it comes to life, reality is the hardest thing there is. When it comes to writing, reality, or faking reality is the easiest. It's so fucking easy. Enough of my ranting," Standing, he glanced around the bar. "This place is like a grave. I'm going to take a piss. If she's not here when I get back—Dog and Cat are getting lonely and need to be fed. And who knows what Dog will have done to that poor idiot while I've been gone."

As Jake walked away, John anxiously checked his phone and again texted Sheila to no avail. He took another drink.

Jake walked back, sat down and reflexively glanced at his watch.

"Good news," John lied. "Sheila texted. She found her phone. She's on her way. She'll be here in fifteen minutes. I promised her we'd stay put."

Jake skeptically stared at John's phone.

"I'll then make it a quick, painless interview and you can go off to read with Cat and Dog." John checked his watch.

"A watch?" Jake said, leaning over and tapping on John's wrist. "I thought your generation's phone was your all-purpose boy scout knife."

"I like the feel of a watch," John replied. "I feel kinda naked without it. She's on her way," he added reassuringly. Forcing a smile, he looked like a fisherman who realized he was just about to lose his catch. "Another beer on me," he said, sneaking a quick peak at his phone and then signaling to the waitress holding up two fingers. "Tell me about the girl."

"What girl?"

"The girl in the colored dress."

Jake nodded but remained silent.

John ran his hand through his hair, gathered up his strength, and forged on. "I'm curious. Why was it life-changing?" He paused and added, "If Sheila's not here when you finish, we'll call it a night."

Jake frowned. He picked up his pen, glanced at John, turned his napkin over, scribbled on it for a bit, then placed it back down. He took a deep breath and glanced around the room, locked his hands behind his head and sat back. "I didn't see her again until 1979 or '80. About fourteen years after my spin at POP. I was in Venice at Beyond Baroque. You ever been there?"

John shook his head. "I've read about it though. That's where Exene met John Doe, right?"

"It's still around, on Venice Boulevard," Jake continued, ignoring John's question. "Been there since the late '60s. Some of the Beats hung out there. They used to have nights when anyone could read their work. Probably still do. They were mostly incomprehensible, dreadful, rambling poems back then. At least mine were. That night I just went to listen. Whatever—after the readings were over everyone was milling, drinking wine, pontificating. A lot of pontificating went on there. Then I saw it. The dress. It was floral, a short summer dress of red, yellow, and blue. It had yellow daisies with blue buds. And that night, in the crowd, there it was. The woman wearing it was attractive, blonde, thin, somewhat pixie-like. I doubted she was the same one from fifteen years back, but I followed her, trying not to look like a stalker. I gulped down a glass of the wine—they always had cheap wine, which was a good thing—collected myself and walked over to her. I said something clever, along the lines of, "I couldn't help noticing your dress."

"'This?' she replied looking down at her dress with a smile. 'It's ancient. I've had it for years. Decades. Can't even think why I wore it. Probably because everything else was dirty. But thank you for noticing.'"

"I nodded, 'Were you possibly wearing it on August 15, 1966 at around 2 pm at Pacific Ocean Park in Venice?'"

"She just stared at me with a confused expression and asked, 'How would I know where I was on August 15, 1966 at 2 pm, much less what I was wearing?'"

"'If it was you, you might remember,' I forged on. 'Did you have an, uh... romantic encounter with the guy who worked that centrifugal force spinning ride at POP, while wearing that dress?'"

"Again, she stared at me, put her hand to her mouth, and burst out laughing. 'How would you know that? You some kind of bizarre literary psychic? They paying you to work the room?'"

"'I was stuck on that ride while you two were... enjoying each other's company.'"

"'Ohmygod!' she cried. 'Are you the one who complained? Paul was fired after that ride. But still, how the hell did you...'"

"'Wasn't me,' I replied. 'I could barely walk, much less complain. I wanted to punch him but staying upright took all my energy. As we spun hopelessly around, I focused on your dress. Each revolution, that was my anchor. That's what kept me from totally disintegrating.'"

"'Sorry,' she said. 'I didn't know. Believe me. I had no idea... well I'm lying. I did. But it didn't seem to take that long, it's just one thing lead to another and before we knew it... See,' she said, leaning towards me conspiratorially, 'it was a bet. He bet me a hundred dollars that I'd never do that at the park, in broad daylight. That little alleyway gave us some cover, so...' She paused and then smiled. 'I knew there was a good chance we'd be caught. But hey, back then a hundred dollars was really a hundred dollars and doing it like that, in the open at the park... well it was a bit of a turn on. And, so you don't get the wrong idea, I wasn't getting paid for having sex. Paul and I had sex all the time. The hundred dollars was for winning the bet.'"

"I laughed and motioning for her to follow, walked over to the table with the wine and poured us each a glass. 'A blow job would have been alright.' I said, clinking my glass to hers. 'That, I assume, would have been over relatively soon, but each time I looked, you two were on to something else—the Kama Sutra at POP. Then, I started thinking and, considering the way basic male anatomy works, each time you two gave something else a try it was going to take a bit longer. That's when the panic began to set in because I figured I could be stuck there for quite a long time. It was then I started to focus on this dress.' I took a bit of the sleeve between my fingers and studied it. 'On each turn, I'd try to find something I missed on the last turn. By the end of that ride, I knew this dress intimately.' I paused and let go of the sleeve. 'So, you end up marrying that guy and have a bunch of POP Karma Sutra kids at home?'"

"'Ha,' she replied, staring down at the dress as she spoke. 'That was the last time I saw him. He said I was the reason that he got fired and that I owed him his hundred dollars back, seeing that he wasn't making money anymore. I told him that he was an ungrateful bastard and that there were plenty of guys who would have paid way more than a hundred dollars. He said that he didn't pay the hundred dollars for the sex, that he'd never pay a woman for sex, and that the hundred dollars was for the bet. But that since it caused him to lose his job that the bet was no longer valid and that I owed him the hundred dollars back.'"

"'So, did you give it back?'"

"'Hell no!'"

"'You still have it? Keep it as a memento?'"

"'The hundred?' she asked with a cock of her head. 'It didn't last through the night, as I recall. You still recovering from that ride of over twenty years ago?'"

"I shrugged and took a drink. 'Been spinning ever since. But that dress was my anchor, so now that it's back things are better. Maybe I can just stare at it to feel stable.'"

"'Be my guest. But I have to warn you, it tends to go where I go,' she said with a grin."

"'Right,' I replied, 'but just to set the record straight, I'm just following the dress. I'm not a stalker or anything like that. Never thought I'd see it again.'"

"'Your lucky day.' She then put down her wine glass. 'Well, the dress is leaving now.' With that she turned and headed towards the exit."

"And you followed the dress?" John asked.

"Didn't really have a choice," Jake replied. "She walked about two blocks to a shiny candy-apple red Corvette. Rally wheels, fifteen-inch tires, AM/FM radio, front and rear speakers, telescoping tilt steering wheel, disc brakes, dual exhaust system—a beauty. And she just very matter-of-factly walked up to it, took the key out of her purse, got in, leaned over, opened the passenger door and waited. I walked over, bent down, stared in, and there was my flowered dress, attached to this seductive blonde sitting in a cherry-red vet.

I stared at her, at the dress, at the car, and instinctively looked up and down the street. Venice was a bit rough around the edges in those days. This was decades before the Silicon Beach invasion. It was the Venice where people went to buy their dope and then sped away. A lone, sexy blonde in a shiny candy-apple red car invited nothing good in that neighborhood. I looked back inside. She leaned over and rolled down the window. "Nice car," I said.

"'Get in,' she directed. 'This dress is pulling away and it would hate to leave you stranded. We need to be formally introduced now, right? I'm Cindy.'"

"I got in and shut the door. 'Jake,' I said. 'My car is a couple of blocks south.'"

"She nodded, started the car and drove west. 'What do you say we grab a quick bite, while you reconnect with the dress?'"

"I laughed."

"She drove to Fisherman's Village." Jake paused and looked at John. "You ever been there?"

John stared up thoughtfully, as though trying to give a different reply. "No."

"Didn't think so. Maybe she drove there because it was the closest we could come to POP. It's on the water, south of the marina. I guess we could have gone to the Santa Monica pier. There was the merry go round, but it was nothing like it is today. I think we both wanted to stay on the south side of the pier. That's what POP celebrated. North was gentrification. Now south is gentrification on steroids. Back then Santa Monica was upscale money and Venice was street. There was an electric sense of life, around-the-corner danger. And southwest of Venice sat, and probably still sits, this touristy little pseudo-fishing village somehow lost in time." Jake paused and smiled.

"We went to one of those fish restaurants," he continued. "One of those touristy places with pictures of nautical scenes and large fake swordfish on the walls. Cindy asked me to sit next to her instead of sitting on the other side, like most people do. I slid in and we ordered fish and chips and two beers."

"'My dress is glad you found her,' Cindy said."

"'Made my decade,' I replied."

"She then leaned into me and kissed me. I kissed her back and we quickly progressed to more serious deep diving. She was leaning against me hard, pushing. I felt I was going to be shoved out of the booth and onto the floor. So, I leaned and pushed back. She seemed to take that as a dare, laughed, took my head in her hands and lowered it towards her left breast. At that point the waitress came over with the manager. He just growled and said if we wanted to do that we should go rent a room and not do it in his restaurant. He accused us of putting on a disgusting display. He then informed us that we had ten seconds to get out of there.

"I protested that our dinner hadn't arrived yet and he snapped that there was no dinner and that we now had five seconds to leave. I started flashing on the scene at the end of *Giant* where the owner of the diner beats the hell out of Rock Hudson. I realize that was about his half-Mexican grandkid and all, but you know what I mean. Rock got the shit kicked out of him and I was afraid that was going to happen to me." Jake paused. "You seen *Giant?*"

John shook his head.

Jake nodded. "I grabbed Cindy by the arm and started to pull her out of the booth. As she slid out, she pulled away from me, marched towards the manager, stopped about a foot away from him and just glared. Her face was beet red. Then, the next thing I know she was screaming. I mean screaming, really screaming, sonic boom volume, saying that we were God-fearing Americans and it was our right to eat in any fucking restaurant we chose and that he had no right to throw us out.

"For good measure, she threw in that her father was a criminal lawyer, had connections with some dangerous people, and that he could arrange a visit. And I mean she's not just saying this, she's threatening at high volume. I took hold of one of her arms and was trying to pull her away, when she began flailing her other arm around like a wild drunken windmill. The manager was big and I could see his fists clenching. He turned, walked to the phone, and called the cops.

"I dragged her out of the restaurant, held her by both arms and gently shook her until she calmed down. 'We gotta get out of here,' I said. 'Give me the car keys.' She nodded, grabbed her keys out of her purse, handed them to me. I took her by the hand and we ran full-tilt back to her car. I put her in the passenger's seat, jumped in and sped off. She was silent for a few seconds and then turned towards me and very matter-of-factly said that she was going to tell her dad about what happened and have some of his associates teach that restaurant owner some manners."

"'What exactly does your dad do?' I asked."

"'I don't want to talk about my dad,' she snapped."

"'You brought him up, so I'm curious.'"

"'Curious about what?'"

"'Your dad, these mysterious friends of his.'"

"'They're not mysterious. They're scary.'"

"'And your dad?'"

"'I told you,' she said, her voice again sliding up in volume, 'I don't want to talk about him.'"

"'What's he like?'"

"She glared at me, looking as though she was holding her breath. She then repeated, the volume rising sharply up as she spoke. 'I told you I don't want to fucking talk about my dad!'"

"'Yeah, I got it,' I said trying to act nonchalant, as though this was a normal conversation."

"'I don't like to be pushed when it comes to my dad and all,' she said her voice gliding back to a normal range. 'Maybe you're right. Maybe I do need to talk about him.' She then paused and added, 'sometime.'"

"'And maybe not,' I said, 'Maybe we just drive, okay? No talking.'"

"She sighed loudly, slid down in the seat, put her feet up on the dashboard, and looked out the window.

"We drove back to Venice in silence. I peeked over every now and then. Her eyes were closed and she looked to be asleep. I parked next to my car and, very gingerly, shook her awake. She wasn't waking up, so I finally had to give her a real shake. She opened her eyes and sat up looking totally disoriented. She shook her head as if to get her bearings, smiled, leaned towards me and kissed me on the cheek. She then opened the car door and exited. I would have married her right there and then."

John frowned, shook his head and sat back in his chair. "But... she seemed a bit unbalanced, disturbed, don't you think?"

"At best," Jake said and took a drink. "I wanted to take her hand, get down on one knee. I almost start crying just thinking about it."

"You're kidding, right?" John asked.

"What I did, was turn off the engine and slide out of her shiny red Vet. She walked over to me and kissed me on the mouth." Jake paused, picked his pen off the table and pointed it at John as one would a dagger. "None of this is on the record, you follow?"

John nodded. "This is just you and me talking at a bar."

Jake nodded and placed his pen back on the table.

"So, she kissed you and left?"

"She kissed me and as I exited the car, she slid into the driver's seat. Looking up at me she smiled and said, 'Get in. This is going to be a long night. We're starting at Blackie's and then work our way east. It's going to be fucking crazy tonight. Everybody's playing.' She waited while I stood there staring down. She then banged on the dashboard and yelled, 'Come on. Get in. We gotta get going!'"

"'Blackie's?' I asked, as I got into the passenger seat."

"Cindy sighed aloud, opened the door, got out, motioned for me to follow her, and marched towards the back of the car. She opened the trunk and waved her arm like one of those girls who show the prizes on game shows. It was filled with camera equipment. 'You follow now?' She asked, closing the trunk and hurrying back to the car. 'We have a lot of ground to cover tonight,' she said. 'I have an assignment for the Music Connection and one for Trouser Press. If it's a good night, I'll be able to place some of the shots in Rolling Stone. We'll start in Santa Monica and work our way to Hollywood.'"

"'You're a photographer?' I asked, jumping in and closing the door."

"'Good call, Sherlock,' she laughed as she started the car and pealed out at an uncomfortably fast speed. 'I shoot rock bands. You can refer to me as a professional photo music journalist.'"

"'Cool.'"

"'Oh, I'm much more than cool, think dry ice.'"

"I wasn't quite sure how to take that. 'I once wrote a piece on Bowie for the *Evening Outlook*,' I offered. 'A while ago. He was still Ziggy then.'"

"'You write?'"

"'Naw. Just that one article,' I said, almost apologetically."

"'You interviewed Bowie?'"

"I shook my head. 'Just a concert review. No pay, but...'"

"'Fucking cool!' she said. 'I'm a photographer and you're a writer. We're a team!'"

"'That's the only piece I ever wrote. Can't really call me a writer.'"

"'I just did.'"

"I nodded."

"'Good,' she said. 'You're a writer. I'm a photographer. I have connections and can get you assignments. I can shoot exclusive photos to accompany your articles.' She paused, and shifting gears as she sped towards Lincoln Boulevard yelled, 'Kismet!'"

Jake paused and took a drink. "This was the late ′70s early ′80s. All pretty much a blur, during the whole punk new wave bit. Disco was raging, but I tried to pretend that didn't exist. I was allergic to that music. Caused a horrible physical reaction. Anyway, as she drove, Cindy explained that she was a rock photographer but not a groupie. Being known as an influential scenester gave her a currency of cool along with access to the clubs, and bands for her photos. At a stoplight she turned to me and proudly announced, 'I also have an assignment for *Velvet*.'"

"'Velvet?' I repeated. 'Velvet like the Velvet Underground?'"

"She laughed. "I wish. It's a skin mag, one of those rags that guys beat-off to. A poor man's *Playboy*, with raunchier girls and more Holland Tunnel shots, pimples and all. Don't pretend you don't know it. I shoot for *Velvet, Gallery, Genesis, Chic,* a bunch of them. Unlike the rock mags, these rags actually pay. They like to look hip, cool so it doesn't seem like guys are just buying their mags to jack-off—even though they are. They need writers,' she added, turning to me and grinning, 'and, like I said—they actually pay.'"

"'Hard to beat.' I replied."

"'Interesting choice of words,' she said with a smile, 'but yeah, you're right. Put on your seat belt. We're heading deep into L.A.'s rock jungle and going to launch your career as a writer.'"

Jake picked up his pen, wrote on the napkin, paused, and placed the pen back on the table. "And she did. She opened the door for me to write for *Trouser Press*, *Cream*, *Rolling Stone*, but also gave me an intro to all of the men's magazines. And like she said, they paid. The rock rags give me street cred and the men mags let me pay my rent and buy groceries."

"That's how you started writing?" John asked.

"That's how I started getting *paid* for writing," Jake corrected. "Had been writing for a while. Some awful stuff published in poetry journals. Some short stories published, but no pay. Cindy was the start of that. My ground zero." He paused and took a drink. "That night it seemed that she was covering the entire L.A. rock scene. It was like a frenzied carnival ride." Jake checked his watch. "These off-the-record ramblings aren't doing you much good. And it looks as though we both might have been stood up. Let's call it a night."

"Sheila's on her way," John said, striking as assured a tone as possible. "This is cool. I love the music from that era. Feel I missed out."

"I promised Sheila I'd sit here for two hours. It fulfills the terms of my contract, so here I sit. Doesn't mean you have to." He paused, as if giving John time to reconsider. He then shrugged and continued. "If I remember, the Gears were playing at Blackies in Santa Monica. I liked that club. It was small, bare bones. Just was what it was. On Main Street, I think. That was before money hit Main. Mostly bars. Straight bars, gay bars, drag bars, dives galore. Cindy parked in a red zone, jumped out, ran to the back, popped open the trunk, grabbed her cameras, told me what to carry, and in we ran. We did a quick check-in, Cindy said her hellos, took some photos of the band, and we were off. I think we next went to the Londoner on Lincoln, an English pub turned new wave rock venue. Not far from a Denny's I think. I don't remember who was there. It was another in-and-out. We then sped up Wilshire Boulevard to Madame Wong's West. Esther Wong owned that place along with the original Madame Wong's in Chinatown. They had both been traditional Chinese restaurants. Someone convinced Esther to let rock bands play at the Chinatown restaurant and there you have it; Madame Wong became a rock impresario. Most all of the new wave bands who played in L.A. played there at one time or another. The Police played there."

"Awesome," John said and cringed.

Jake paused. Glared at John, who nodded apologetically, and continued. "Anyway, Cindy parked. By now we had our system down and we grabbed her photo equipment out of the trunk and hurried towards the front entrance of Madame Wong's. I ran after her. I seemed to always be running after Cindy. She never walked. Life moved too fast for her or not fast enough. Never did figure that out. 'You gotta keep up, if you wanna make it,' she yelled. Not sure what 'it' she was talking about. The bouncer at the door knew her, smiled and waved for her to pass. He glowered at me, blocking my way until she turned and said, 'He's cool. He's with me.' Begrudgingly he stood aside, allowing me to enter."

"The club was packed. The Naughty Sweeties were headlining. They were a huge draw, but I don't think they were ever deemed cool enough to secure a record deal. Which was strange considering that those were the days when Electra, A&M, Geffen, Dream, I.R.S., Chrysalis and others were falling all over themselves, signing just about any band that could play three chords. Bands could make money selling music back then," Jake added. "An archaic concept."

"Cindy snaked me through the crowd and into a small office. Esther, aka Madame Wong, was there and her eyes lit up when they spied Cindy and her camera. Esther loved cameras. Danny Elfman, the Oingo Boingo guy, and Martha Davis of the Motels and her daughter were in the office. Cindy beamed as she entered. She knew photos of those three together would sell. 'You're a star, Esther!' Cindy exclaimed and gave her a hug. She then went to work, directing and posing everyone. She was a natural. She'd command and all obeyed. That was the amazing part—everyone did whatever Cindy told them to. 'These photos are great,' she announced, 'I'll get them placed everywhere.'"

"And that's what Esther loved. Cindy got Esther's picture published and Esther gave Cindy free reign of both clubs, free to shoot whomever she wanted to. There were articles on Esther being the queen of punk, but, to be honest, she had nothing to do with punk. She hated punk music, not that she could tell the difference between one band to another. Punk bands wouldn't adhere to Wong's rules, so she simply wrote them off. The Hong Kong Café in Chinatown was where the punk bands played. It was right across from Madame Wong's. She had a policy that if she found out a band played at the Hong Kong Cafe, that was it, they were banned from Madame Wong's for life. You didn't fuck with Esther.

"I stood in the background watching as Cindy choreographed her photos. She then turned to me and announced, 'Esther, this is Jake. He writes for *Rolling Stone*, *Cream*, *Trouser Press*, the *L.A. Times*, you name it, he writes for them and he wants to do a story on you.'"

"I simply stared at Cindy as I stood rigid, rooted to the floor.

"Esther was diminutive with a short black mop-top and a

perpetual frown. She stared at me and the frown lifted as she said, '*Rolling Stone*. You write article on me for *Rolling Stone*.'"

"'You got it,' Cindy exclaimed. 'But not now. Not tonight. We gotta go take some shots of the show now. Speaking of, let me take one of you two together.' Cindy positioned me next to Esther. 'Put your arm around her,' she ordered. I did as commanded and Esther and I smiled as the camera flashed. 'Perfect,' Cindy said. 'That's a cover. Okay, we're off.'"

"'*Rolling Stone*,' Esther repeated, more as a command than a question.'"

"'Right,' I replied, saying it more as a question than a statement."

"Elfman looked confused. As though he wasn't sure he'd done the right thing—'I can get a copy of those photos, right?' he asked. 'You'll let me okay them and let me know where you're sending them.'"

"'Sure,' Cindy replied off-handedly. She then grabbed my hand and rushed me towards the door. 'Not,' she softly added as she pulled me along and guided me through the bodies to the main stage."

"The opening band was called Skirtz. Three female singers backed by a power pop trio. The Supremes meet The Who. They were still finishing their set and Cindy said we couldn't wait, so she rounded up the members of the Sweeties and had them pose backstage. 'I love you guys, but we need to get to the Starwood, the Whisky, and the Hong Kong before the night's over.'"

"'The best show is going to be here though,' replied one of the Sweeties' members."

"'Don't think I don't know that,' she said, packing up her camera. 'And by the way, this is Jake, he's on assignment for *Rolling Stone*.'"

"I tried to give a nonchalant nod."

"'*Rolling Stone*?' the band said in unison."

"'I'll make sure he catches your act. But now we gotta run,' she said. The lead singer began to speak, but Cindy yelled, 'Bye,' grabbed my hand, and pulled me down the stairs and back into the Santa Monica night."

"'They all think I write for *Rolling Stone*,' I said, as I ran after her towards her car."

"'Well, you probably do now,' she replied, opening her trunk and placing her camera equipment inside. 'Like I said, I have connections. My shots have been published in *Rolling Stone*. Why not your articles? Plus, think of my declaration as a form of creative visualization. Read the book. If you declare it as having happened, it will. Hurry up, get in. We're late.'"

"I did and we sped away, driving east on Wilshire, south on Sepulveda and then east on Pico. She drove at a speed that would have had every cop in the city on me. Our next stop was the Starwood in Hollywood on Santa Monica Boulevard. The club booked a mix of punk bands like Fear and X, and Black Flag, along with more pop groups like the Plimsouls and the Go-Go's."

Jake paused, took a drink, picked up his pen, made some notes on the napkin, placed the pen back down. "What the fuck am I doing sitting here telling you stories that you can't use?"

"We're waiting for Sheila, who will be here any second," John replied. "Besides, this is great stuff. Why don't you write about this?"

"I told you. I write fiction."

"I've always been taught that writers should write what they know."

"Bullshit," Jake said. "Do you know how many great books we wouldn't have if writers stuck to what they knew? It's called fucking fiction!" he exclaimed, slamming his hand against the table, causing John to jump back and everyone at the bar to turn and stare. "God that pisses me off. Why did you have to bring that up?"

"I didn't mean to," John apologized, quickly glancing at his phone.

Jake sighed, held up his hand and motioned towards the waitress. "Another beer for my exceedingly patient interviewer," he called out. "Now, Johnny," he said, picking up his pen and putting it in his pocket, "I'm going to leave you here and head home. When Sheila arrives, remember, she owes you for putting you through this. Let her know that in your anger, you could write a horrific piece of slander about me and my books. You could single-handedly ruin a career she's worked years to build."

"I would never do that," John said, a hurt expression on his face.

"Hint that there is a way this horrific story could get squashed," Jake added with a glint, "that she has the power to make it all go away."

John shook his head and took a drink. "You always pimp out your rep like this? She works hard for you, you know. She's got your back more than most."

"Precisely," Jake said with a nod. "If I thought you seriously had designs on Sheila, things would not go so well for you. But—I like you."

John smiled uneasily. "So," he asked, "the Go-Go's were at the Starwood that night?"

Jake laughed. "Persistence."

"She's almost here. Plus, I'm really interested in this."

Jake nodded, took a drink, pulled his pen out of his pocket and placed it back on the table. "That night Wall of Voodoo was opening for the Go-Go's. Again, Cindy got us past the door guards, or bouncers or whatever you call them, and up the stairs we went. Wall of Voodoo was in mid-set. They were good. I wanted to stay and watch, but Cindy grabbed my arm and pulled me along until we came to the dressing room. Again the bouncers, recognizing Cindy, parted and let us pass. Everyone let Cindy pass. The room was filled with hangers-on talking, drinking, smoking. The Go-Go's were preparing to go on. They all knew Cindy and laughed as they gave hello hugs. No sooner were we in the room than she was directing, barking out orders, and going ready-aim-shoot. I watched as a long leggy girl walked up to another girl, pulled up her blouse pushed her against the wall and started sucking on her tits. And that girl had amazing tits. I'll never forget those tits. I turned to see if Cindy would shoot it. She watched for a few seconds, shrugged, laughed and went back to shooting the band.

"I was the only guy backstage. Tried to act nonchalant, as though it was all perfectly normal. Another day in the life. The Go-Go's all seemed to be in a pretty up mood. They had signed with I.R.S. records. I think Kathy had just joined the band after being kicked out of the Textones. I don't remember, but the mood seemed upbeat. And Cindy plugged in to it. She was a pro. No male photographer would have gotten the photos she did. I doubt another female would. It was Cindy. One of the beefy steroided bouncers stuck his head in, announced that they were up and the band grabbed their gear, and headed towards the stage.

"It was disorienting, like the POP ride all over again, felt as though the floor had given way and I was being pushed by speed force, but this time there was no wall to lean against and no one could see me spinning. I was twirling away all by myself. Spinning like one of those Fourth of July fireworks that screech and rush haphazardly around until they flame out. I grabbed a can of beer off the table that someone left behind and chugged it down hoping that would normalize things a bit. Cindy gave the band goodbye hugs. As I hurried after Cindy, the girl with the amazing tits smiled at me as she walked out with one of those you-know-you-want-me grins. And, she was right. Cindy waited for me to catch up and grabbed my arm. 'We gotta go,' she said as she pulled me through the club and out the door."

"'We're going to miss their set,' I protested, as she pulled me towards the car."

"'This isn't playtime, you know,' she barked, as she opened the trunk and carefully placed in her photo equipment. 'This is work. I'm on the clock.'"

"'But I've never seen the Go-Go's.'"

"'Don't whine! I hate it when guys whine. We gotta go. Now!' she said, jumping into the car and starting the motor. 'Hurry. Belinda was bummed because something big is happening tonight at the Blue Lagoon Saloon and they were going to miss it. If she's right, this night could be big.' Cindy turned and smiled at me. 'You could be my lucky charm.'"

"'I could have told you that,' I replied as I climbed into the passenger's seat. 'You should have shot that gal with her tits out.'"

"'That got to you, didn't it?' she shook her head. 'Guys are so easy.'"

"I shrugged."

"She leaned over, grabbed the beer out of my hand, finished it and tossed it out the car window. 'You're not supposed to drink beer outside,' she chided. 'It's illegal.' She then put the car in gear and headed back to the westside. 'I took shots of all of this other girl band in bed once,' she said, as though picking up a conversation we had started earlier. 'They thought it was funny, but their management and label found out about it and I started to get death threats on my answering machine. This very angry male voice said if those photos and negatives were not delivered to the management company immediately, and if they ever appeared in any publications, that I wouldn't be around much longer. Implied something very bad would happen. Stupid someone leaving that kind of threat on an answering machine, eh? But this guy did. Twice!'"

Jake took a drink and turned towards John. "You gotta remember this was the early '80s. People still had answering machines. Still took pictures with cameras, with film. Destroy the film, the negatives, and poof, the photos disappear. Forever. Like they never existed. Disappearing is a lost luxury. Now everyone is a walking recording device and once an image gets on to the internet it's there—forever. Now every image, every keystroke, pretty much every action is recorded. Saved forever and ever, amen. Back then *1984* was still a futuristic book. It seems quaint now. That train whizzed by a long time ago.'" He paused. "Where was I?"

"You were going to some place called the Blue Lagoon," John said, covertly checking his watch, hoping to keep Jake talking until Sheila arrived; checking the door, and imagining he saw Sheila walking in.

"Right. You ever go there?" Jake asked.

John shook his head.

"Disappeared a long time ago. On Lincoln Boulevard, right where Venice ended and Marina del Rey began. It was close to an Irish pub that had turtle races." Jake paused. "Funny, I'd forgotten all about those turtle races. Anyway, I tried to focus as Cindy drove from Santa Monica Boulevard to Fairfax to the 10 freeway to Lincoln Boulevard where she went south to the Blue Lagoon. I never much liked driving that stretch of Lincoln from Pico to the Marina. A cold concrete, seedy steely feel to it. She seemed to be driving a hundred miles an hour between stoplights, talking and laughing as she drove. She was having fun and I was clutching on to the door, preparing for imminent death.

"We finally get there and Cindy found a place to park on the street. It was old hat to me by then. I hopped out, helped her grab her equipment and once again, she was pulling me along as we rushed towards the club. We raced up the stairs and towards the bouncers who grinned at Cindy and parted to let us pass. I was now getting used to being introduced as a writer for *Rolling Stone*. By this time, I think I had been promoted to senior editor. Everyone loved me. Everyone wanted to know me. I wasn't simply anybody but somebody and I was everybody's best friend. It was a strange site for a rock venue, particularly after the Starwood. Had a very Polynesian South Seas vibe to it. 20/20 was on stage. For once, Cindy actually allowed me to watch the band play. Then Doug Fieger comes on stage and..."

"Who?" John asked.

"Fieger. Doug Fieger. The lead singer for the Knack. You know, 'My Sharona.'"

John frowned thoughtfully. He then smiled and nodded. "Oh yeah. That song. That song was in some film, right?"

Jake grunted and continued. "Then I think the Plimsouls came on stage, followed by Fast Freddy and then some musicians I didn't know, but Cindy was jumping up and down, exclaiming 'Yes!' so I figured they must have been someone. They all started jamming together and Cindy, punched me on the shoulder and yelled, 'You're my good luck charm. These are money shots!' She bought me a beer in thanks. I was getting pretty buzzed by that point. There was this quasi mosh pit down by the stage. It was basically mosh-pit-light. That real stuff was downtown, X, Fear, Black Flag territory. But at that point I didn't give a shit. I rushed down, threw myself in and was banging against all of these people I never met and having a hell of a time. If you did that anywhere else you'd be in an automatic fist fight, but here it was all human bumper cars. Thrashing and flying into everyone else was the whole point. And that made me feel normal. The music and banging and screaming all matched what was going on inside my head. And when the bands stopped playing, I was as drenched as if I'd walked into the ocean fully clothed. I found a wall to lean against and stood there trying to regain my bearings. Cindy found me, grabbed my arm and, once again, pulled me along. I was kind of like her pet, or pull toy; she pulled and I followed. Then there we were backstage again. It was cool, a who's who of the L.A. new wave scene along with some young up-and-coming actors who were looking to gain some rock street cred."

"This dark-haired girl walks up to me and says. 'Hi, maybe you've heard of me, my name is Sharona.' I paused and said, 'No I don't think so,' and Cindy elbows me and says, 'Don't be dense. She's Sharona, you know, SHARONA.' And I said something lame like, 'Oh yeah, cool.' And the dark-haired girl smiled, accepted my acknowledgement and drifted away."

"Cindy was busy working the room. Moving and positioning as many rock stars, wanna-be rock stars, and trendy hangers on as possible. Mashing them in photos together."

"Were you in any?" John asked.

"I wasn't anybody. No reason for me to be in the shots."

"Too bad. Those would be worth money now. Besides I thought you were senior editor of *Rolling Stone* by then."

"No one ever told me I'd be anyone, so I never prepared for it," Jake explained, a pensive expression on his face. "Take that as a lesson. Anyway, there was this one guy, a real new wave fashion plate—a dedicated follower of fashion, as the song goes. He was a singer in some band. Don't remember their name; had a lot of hangers-on swimming around him. Dolled up, very Mod, affecting an uber cool vibe. Had a throwback Beatles haircut, but styled. As Cindy and I walked by, he said something along the lines of, 'Yeah, girl bands are fun to look at. The Go-Go's and all. Kinda like a carnival, but they don't have anything to do with rock and roll.' He paused and then added, 'Girls are good for three things.' He then burst out laughing and his tribe chirped in accordingly. Cindy came to a hard stop, which had me walk into her. She then marched up to him and asked—well, more demanded than asked—'Yeah? What three things are girls good for?'"

"He paused, looked down at her and glanced back at his entourage and, as if on cue, they all turned towards Cindy and burst out laughing. He then just glared at her and pointedly announced, 'Mouth, pussy and ass.'"

"Cindy's expression remained stone-like as she let her camera drop and rest on the shoulder strap. 'So… that's it, huh?'"

"'Pretty much sums it up,' he said. Again, laughter followed."

"'And you… you and your band… you guys play real rock and roll?'"

"'Yep.'"

"'And you're like better than the Pretenders?'"

"'Probably,' he said matter-of-factly. 'Why do you think they're called the Pretenders?'"

"Again, laughter."

"Cindy moved closer. Her speech was coming out more quickly, louder, higher pitched. She was speaking with a machine gun delivery. 'And Patti Smith?' she shot, 'you're saying Patti Smith can't fucking play rock and roll? You're saying her fucking rendition of Gloria is not rock and roll?'"

"'Patti Smith?' He repeated with a sour expression. 'Who in their right mind would want to fuck Patti Smith?'"

"'Forget fucking!' she commanded. 'You're saying she can't play rock and roll?'"

"He turned again and looked at his troupe with a 'can you believe this?' expression. 'Yeah. I'm saying just that. She can't play rock and roll. I'm saying she's a fucking joke.'"

"While he was talking, Cindy bent down and put her camera equipment carefully on the ground. She then stood back up, her spine straight, fists clenched. 'You're saying Patti Smith is a joke?'"

"'A joke. A loser. She's nothing.'"

"'Patti Smith is nothing?' she yelled, causing people to turn and Sharona to glide back our way to see what the commotion was."

"'Nothing,' he repeated with a practiced Sid Vicious sneer. 'She's shit.'"

"And with that Cindy hauled off, slamming her fist into his face. He reeled and almost fell. He then cried, 'You fucking bitch!' and let go with a wild swing. Cindy weaved out of the way, impressively, I might add. He missed her but caught Sharona on the side of her face and she let go with a blood curdling scream and hit the ground with a thud. Then Fieger turned around, saw his Sharona on the floor, and flew on top of this guy swearing non-stop as he was pounding him in the face. Then some of the guy's friends went to pull Fieger off and somebody hit one of them. And it was as if I was watching a '50s western brawl scene. More and more people joined in and it turned into a free-for-all. Cindy grabbed my hand, backed us out, and started taking photos. 'These are great!' she said with a cheerful smile. 'These shots are my best... ever.' She then pulled me towards the stairs and out of the club.'"

"Laughing, we ran to the car. I was pleasantly high at that point. We laughed about seeing My Sharona decked. I stared out the window watching the concrete shopping malls of Lincoln Boulevard give way to the tonier stores of Santa Monica. She took a slight detour heading west to Palisades Park and then north on Main Street. To our left were the bluffs and beyond them the Pacific Ocean. People strolled on the park which overlooked the darkness of the sea. Palm trees stood as silent sentries. Cindy went east onto Montana Boulevard, passing the small upscale shops to the expanse of San Vicente Boulevard. Then north on some street I didn't know through winding streets past the quiet, moneyed homes and manicured lawns of Brentwood.

"She drove into the horseshoe driveway of a very upscale, impeccably landscaped home. It was set on a tree-lined street, behind a white picket fence, one of those quintessential east coast traditionals. She parked, exited, and took her gear out of the trunk. I think I simply sat there and stared at the house. She motioned to me to follow and I did. We entered into something that looked more like a movie set than an actual home. She took my hand and walked me through the formal entry with adjacent powder room, then into the living room which had a large stone fireplace that opened onto a spacious family/game room with wet bar, which had its own raised brick fireplace. Then to the kitchen with a spacious breakfast room, formal dining room, study/office, and guest room. Each room looked like a page out of *Architectural Digest*. She then led me up the stairs to a large master suite with a fireplace and a huge bay window that looked out over a yard complete with Jacuzzi and Olympic-sized pool."

"'Your dad does okay,' I said, as she sat me on the bed and began to unbutton my shirt.'"

"'He does,' she laughed, 'but he doesn't live here.'"

"'Whose is this?' I asked. 'I mean, is it okay we're here?'"

"'It's mine,' she answered matter-of-factly. 'And yes, it's okay you're here. I give you permission.'"

"Confused, I nodded silently. She finished undressing me, put my clothes neatly on a large, antique-looking wooden chair, and walked me to a bathroom with double sinks, a sauna, and oversized shower. She then walked out, returned sans the dress and, again taking my hand, led me into the shower. We both laughed as we took turns soaping each other. We dried ourselves using plush oversized pink towels. Cindy steered me to the king-sized bed with an intricately carved wooden frame and we slipped between the sheets. I laughed. She kissed me. I kissed her back. I slid on top of her and we explored one another until we feel asleep.

"When I awoke, I was still a bit woozy. Cindy rolled over towards me, smiled and kissed me. She got up and walked to the kitchen to make us coffee. I looked around the room and called out, asking her how she could afford the place on a photographer's salary. She smiled, replied that she had a roommate and told me to meet her in the kitchen for breakfast.

"I put on my clothes and walked into the kitchen where she stood wearing a form-fitting powder-blue robe, humming as she made us an omelet. Cindy put down the pan, turned off the stove, picked up her coffee and sat down at the breakfast table.

"This place is amazing. How do you afford it? I repeated.

"She looked up and stared at me with a sad, melancholy expression."

"'What's wrong?' I asked."

"'You know what's wrong.' she replied softly."

"'I don't,' I said."

"'You know what's wrong and there's nothing we can do about it.' Placing her hands on a chair, she bent over, lowered her head and began to cry and she kept crying. I tried to think what would so upset a girl so I asked, 'Are you pregnant?'"

"'No, I'm not fucking pregnant,' she snapped, glaring up at me. 'Why would you ask that? And if I was pregnant why would that be so horrible?'"

"'It wouldn't be,' I said, trying to figure out where the conversation was going. 'But I know it can be scary for a girl to be pregnant when she's not married and...'"

"She then straightened up, picked up her cup, took a sip, and turned towards me. 'But I am married.'"

"I laughed. I don't remember if it was a genuine laugh or a nervous reaction. But I laughed."

"'I am married,' she repeated almost defiantly. 'How do you think I can afford this?'"

"I just stared, not knowing what to say. I finally asked. 'Where is he?'"

"'At a medical convention.' She paused and took another sip. 'He'll be back tomorrow.'"

"'He's a doctor?'"

"'You think taking photos would pay for this? You think that would pay for anything?'"

"I just shook my head, still dazed. 'He pays the bills, but he's an asshole, right?' I asked. 'He's like your dad.'"

"'He's kind. He's good to me.' She then paused and added, 'And don't bring up my father. You don't know anything about my father.'"

"'So you're happily married,' I demanded."

"'I said he's kind.'"

"I stood up and walked back into the bedroom to grab my wallet. In my mind, I played one of those exit scenes you see in films. One of those dramatic scenes where the two characters yell at one another and finally, in disgust or despair, one turns and storms out. I splashed water on my face and just stared at myself in the mirror as the water dripped down. Ten minutes before, I was sure she was the one. A bit crazy, a bit out of control, but the one that fit me. I was a galaxy of smiles and then—wham! All gone. A magic trick gone awry, a tablecloth being pulled taking everything down, crashing to the floor. I dried my face, walked back into the kitchen and stared at a spot on the rug. I didn't look at her. Keeping my eyes focused on that spot kept me from looking up and breaking into a thousand pieces. I then turned and walked towards the front door."

"'I can see you next Wednesday night,' she called out, her voice bright and hopeful."

"I stopped, turned, and looked at her. She was smiling with that smile that made me want to just stand there and smile back. But I didn't. I looked away and said, 'You're married.'"

"She nodded."

"'We can't do this if you're married.'"

"'Yes we can.'"

"'I want to be the one who's married to you.' My voice was shaky."

"Her smile grew. 'That is so wonderful. Life has a way of changing. Right now, I'm married. Right now, that's how it is. How it has to be. He's a good guy. You'd like him. Right now, there can be nights like last night. Well, I'm not going to make a habit of hitting people at clubs, but nights we can share. And Wednesday we can have another night and there will be others after that. Take what you can in this life. Take what it offers, or it just keeps going and before you know it, it's gone. I want to see you on Wednesday. That would be special. That would make me happy.'"

"I looked away and finally said, 'I want more.'"

"'Everyone wants more,' she said. 'No one ever has it all. That's a myth. A lie. Take the gifts life gives you. Life gave us last night, this morning, it's giving us Wednesday and will give us more. Let's take life up on it, Jake. Don't give life ultimatums. You never win that way.'"

"'Will you leave him?' I asked, hearing her words fly at me like undecipherable noise."

"'He travels a lot,' she replied, 'to medical conventions and to give lectures. He leaves again on Wednesday. We could go to Fisherman's Village.' She smiled again."

"'I can't,' I said. I then paused and tried to get my feet to walk out the door. Finally, I got one foot to move, followed by the other." Jake stared towards the bar and went silent.

"So… you walked back, all the way from Brentwood to Venice?" John asked.

Jake picked up his beer and took a drink. "My feet didn't want to walk. They liked it where they were." Jake picked up his pen and began to write on the napkin. "I didn't leave," he said, looking up at John. He paused and placed the pen back on the table. "We continued to continue for about a year. She'd call when she was free. My life was basically waiting for her calls. She'd call, I'd jump, and for a few hours I'd be alive. I was a vampire and Cindy was my night. We became regular prowlers of the rock clubs. She shot photos and I wrote articles. I became a paid writer, just as she promised. My stuff started to get picked up, first by the *Music Connection* and the *Reader* and then by *Trouser Press* and *Cream* and eventually I placed that promised piece on Esther Wong in *Rolling Stone*." Jake shook his head and sighed audibly. "To this day I still don't understand why anyone wants to read about what rock stars have to say, but… there you have it. I became a working writer. A journalist," he added somewhat dismissively, "but, still. And, as she predicted, it was writing for the skin mags that kept me afloat. The rock rags gave me street cred and the men's rags paid the bills. I was making my living as a writer, barely eking one out, but still, I was a writer. Cindy did that. I wouldn't have had the confidence to do it on my own. Not back then. She set up the first big interviews—Petty, Elvis Costello, the near Bowie interview. She set up the Burroughs interview. She knew I wanted that one, so she made up a nonexistent magazine assignment. His rep bought it. It was a gift. She was magic, quicksilver, each time I saw her I fell deeper down the rabbit hole. And afterwards I'd erupt, smash things, vow that I'd never see her again and I'd mean it—until the next time she called. When I did see her, life was lighter, crystal bright, electric. Everything shone differently. We had fun.

"Sounds simple, basic, but the laughter was the drug, not the sex or romance or whatever else draws people together. We laughed. We did things I never did on my own or with anyone else. She'd talk about anything, tell me anything, unless it had to do with her father or husband. Apart from those two topics, there were no boundaries, nothing was off limits. It was like a curtain that opened and played this amazing holographic film that we were in. I knew it was unsustainable, but it never felt that way until the curtain closed, until I dropped her off, or she left to go back home. Then the bulb dimmed and darkness fell." Jake looked up and paused. He then continued, as if talking to himself. "I understood jamming a needle into your arm to make it to the next minute."

John shook his head.

"Writing became my junk. It was how I escaped. Created another world. Lost myself there." Jake stopped, stared at John pensively. A sadness came to his face and he continued. "Then one day, I picked her up from a bus stop that we'd sometimes use as our rendezvous, our secret meeting place in plain sight. That day she was glowing, smiling like the sun at high noon. She jumped in the car and I asked her why she was so happy. She leaned over and kissed me on the mouth and proclaimed, 'I am happiness personified!' She'd say things like that. I used to like it. I laughed and drove off. I don't remember what we did. Maybe we went to Zuma beach, or the Redondo Pier, or Chinatown to buy herbs. I don't remember. I figured her husband must have been out of town, because we went to dinner and we only went to dinner if he was out of town. We ended up on Melrose, had dinner at Antonio's. You been there?"

John shook his head.

"You'd make a good monk. Anyway, they make one of the best moles in the city. She didn't like mole. She said it was like eating chicken with a chocolate sundae poured over it. She had a chicken tostada and we both had margaritas. She said that her husband had to go to Europe for a conference. He wanted her to go with him, but she had managed to talk her way out of it. We had the next ten days to ourselves. She announced that she wanted us to go to La Jolla for the weekend. I don't think I replied. I'd never spent more than a night with her, had never gone away with her, and I knew that if I did, I'd just keep falling deeper and deeper and would never be able to crawl out. She then shot me this shining smile and asked, 'You know, right?' she asked."

"'Know what?' I replied."

"'You know,' she repeated, this time as a definitive statement."

"'Know what?'"

"'Don't pretend you don't know,' she said with a laugh. 'You of all people in this entire world would know.'"

"'Cindy,' I replied, getting a bit frustrated by the game. 'I don't know what you're talking about.'"

"'Like it's not written all over my face.' She took a sip of her margarita. 'Like it's not so obvious that the guy who parked the car knows.'"

"I took a deep breath and then slowly repeated, 'Knows what?'"

"She took another drink, slid over towards me in the booth, put her hand on my thigh, and as she squeezed, leaned in to my ear and announced in a loud whisper, 'I'm pregnant!'"

"I was a pinball machine on tilt. The lights on, but everything stuck. I said nothing in response."

"She kissed me on the check, slid back over to her side of the booth, picked up her margarita and holding her glass high proclaimed—'a toast!'"

"'That's not funny.'"

"'Of course, it's funny,' she replied. 'It's funny and fun and amazing and wonderful and it's exactly what I am. I am all of those things rolled into one because—I am pregnant!'"

"My hand shook as I moved the drink to my mouth. I drank until I had emptied the glass."

"'Wow, that is a toast,' she said, 'you finished the whole thing. But we didn't clink our glasses. Didn't really toast.' She waived the waiter over and ordered two more drinks."

"'Whose is it?' I asked in a near whisper."

"She shrugged. 'It's all of ours. It's a soul that wanted to come. And it's coming. That's all that matters.'"

"'Does he know?' I asked."

"She shook her head. 'Not yet. I wanted to tell you first.'"

"'Why?'"

"'I wanted to celebrate. This is a celebration and you're sitting there looking all gloom and doom trying to ruin the whole thing.'"

"'Why would I celebrate the fact that you're pregnant and married and I don't know who's the father and I'm being pushed further and further out of your life?'"

"She took another drink and frowned. 'Why are you acting like this?' she demanded. 'We're starting a new adventure—a soul adventure. Together. You're not being pushed out, you're being brought in. Just think of all the new experiences we'll have together. The three of us. We're heading into the unknown. Billions have done it, but not me, not us; for us this is a first, sailing off the cliff, an adventure into deep spiritual space.'"

"'You're going to keep it?'"

"'She sprang back with an expression that looked as though she'd been hit. 'What a horrible question. That's the most horrible question anyone has ever asked me.'"

"'Whose is it?' I asked again."

"Her eyes began to moisten. 'I thought we were going to celebrate. I thought this was going to be special. I've been planning and waiting for this night for days and all you're doing is being mean and dark and angry.'"

"'Celebrate? Now I'm supposed to steal time and see you with a child that is maybe mine whenever you have time for me? Is that how you see me living my life?'"

"'No!' Cindy said adamantly. She paused and looked away. 'You'll meet somebody. I know that. I've prepared myself for that, but we'll still have us. That doesn't have to change. Who we are is outside of everything else. Our world is exactly that—ours. You know that. This soul needed to come through me. No matter how it came, it's ours—as much yours as mine.'"

"'And what about him?' I asked."

"'What about him?' she snapped. 'He'll be happy. He'll be fucking ecstatic. He won't act like you. He won't be cruel, he won't be cold, mean.'"

"'Of course, he won't,' I said, the volume of my voice matching hers. 'He doesn't know about me. Us. He's in blissful ignorance. He thinks everything is perfect, sure in the knowledge that he's the fucking father. He gets it all. He gets you, the child, he gets to believe everything's perfect. Never has to know the truth.'"

"'I'm with you now, aren't I?'"

"'You're with me because he's gone.'"

"'I'm with you because I want to be with you, at least I did,' she added, finishing her drink. 'I don't understand why you're acting this way.'"

"'I'm beginning to believe you,' I mumbled, speaking mainly to myself."

"'Meaning?'"

"'I'm beginning to believe you really think that this is normal. That this is okay.'"

"'We're not like them,' she said leaning towards me, her eyes widening. 'We're different. Our relationship is different. It's special. The fact that I'm pregnant and with you tonight...' She paused and stared at me. 'You do get it. You know. You've always known. Our fields reach out, expand. When we're together like this it's magic, but when we're apart, we're still together. Don't you see? We're still...' She stopped and then added, 'You get it.'"

"'I don't fucking get anything,' I said coldly. 'I don't have a clue what you're talking about and doesn't drinking hurt the fetus? Aren't you attacking your fucking baby? I'd say stop, but I don't have any rights. I'm the dumb fuck on the side.'"

"Cindy glared at me. She then picked up her drink, paused, and tossed what was left of it in my face. She then slid out of the booth, stood up, and stared down at me. 'Fuck you!' she yelled, her voice dead and bitter. 'Who the fuck are you to talk to me like that? I thought tonight was special. I thought you... I thought you of all people. I thought you'd be...' She stared down at me, her lips quivering, then turned and walked away."

John sat in silence waiting for Jake to finish. He took a drink. He finally asked, "And then?"

"And then nothing," Jake said.

"You didn't go after her?"

"I went to the restroom, washed the drink off my face, and tried to dry my shirt. I returned to the table and finished my mole. The waiter came up and said she was very pretty, but maybe a bit too excitable. That maybe it's good that she's gone."

"'Either way, she's gone.' I said."

"The waiter nodded. 'For good, señor?'"

"I nodded."

"'Then... a margarita on me. A celebration to the future.'"

"I forced a laugh. 'Tonight everyone wants to celebrate and toast to things that are breaking my heart.'"

"He smiled. He had the best smile I've ever seen on a waiter. 'Sometimes a broken heart deserves a toast.'"

"'A philosopher disguised as a waiter.' I said."

"He smiled. 'I'll be right back with your bill.' He walked away and I did my best impersonation of enjoying a meal. He quickly returned, looked down at me and shook his head. 'There is no bill. The señora, she paid for it at the bar before she left. Very cruel.'" Jake paused, picked up his drink and looked away.

John sat through an uncomfortable silence and then asked, "What did you..."

"Let's call it a night," Jake said.

"But the story just can't end there," John continued.

Jake stared at him and looked away. He took a breath that sounded like a sigh, stood and walked to the bathroom.

John stared at his phone saying a silent prayer that a message would appear. Nothing did. "Good news!" he exclaimed, looking up with a smile, as Jake walked back towards the table. "She's just about here," he continued, holding up his phone, as if in evidence, "fifteen minutes away. Says to apologize to you for the screw up." He paused. "How did you move from rock journalism to fiction?"

"You're moving into restricted territory again," Jake replied. He glanced towards the door and sat down.

John nodded. "I know, but... just curious."

Jake sat back, pulled his sunglasses out of his pocket and began to clean the lenses with his napkin. He looked up at John. "It had to do with a woman and a gun." He smiled and slipped his sunglasses back in his shirt pocket.

"That's it?" John asked. He waited. "So" he continued, "the gun, was it fired?"

Jake nodded. "Several times, as I recall."

"You can't just leave it there," John said.

Jake picked up his pen and began to scribble on the napkin. He then looked up at John. "Who'd you vote for?" he asked.

"Come on," John pleaded, "what happened with the gun? How did that lead to you writing? Besides," he added, "I don't talk politics. Only leads to trouble."

"Look what it did for Hunter S. Thompson."

"What happened with the gun?" John again asked. The two sat in silence.

Jake placed his pen carefully on the table. He then looked up. "Can't blame Trump."

John stared at Jake, a disconcerted expression on his face. "You like Trump?"

"He's a hologram. He's not there." Jake looked up and studied those at the bar. The room was filling up now. Standing room only as patrons jockeyed to grab the bartender's attention. "They're there," Jake said with a pointed finger.

John turned and stared at a middle-aged hipster couple at the bar who now seemed to be locked in an argument. "You blaming them?"

"They think in binary terms and binary thinking leads directly to the circle of hell we're in now."

A confused expression on his face, John snuck a look at his phone.

"We're all guilty," he conceded.

Jake shook his head. "Don't drag me into this."

"Like I said, I prefer not to talk politics."

"The guilty never do," Jake said with a victorious nod. "It all comes down to one thing, one person—OJ."

John opened his mouth as if to speak.

"That Bronco ride," Jake continued. "It led to the original televised Kardashian. Daddy Kardashian spawned his minions and they went on to conquer the world. There would have been no *Apprentice* without OJ. He birthed reality TV, which birthed Trump, and here we are."

"It's not that simple."

"There's nothing simple about it," Jake agreed. "But it's fact."

John looked away. He then stared at his watch. "Why not write the story of the girl with the colored dress?"

"Changing the subject is not going to absolve you." Jake pulled his phone out of his pocket and looked down at the screen. "Unknown number," he said. "I never answer those."

"Answer!" John cried, jumping up out of his seat. "It's Sheila. Answer it!" he all but yelled.

"I know Sheila's number, it's not..."

"But she lost her phone. She'll be calling from another number. Answer it!"

Jake raised both eyebrows and answered. "This had better be Sheila," he said. Looking up at John, he nodded. "You don't need to apologize to me, but you'd better damn well apologize to John. He is getting more than a bit testy. Where are you? I thought you told John you were going to be here in fifteen..."

John quickly reached over and grabbed the phone out of Jake's hand. "Sheila," he cried. "Jake's some kidder, right? You okay? I told

Jake that we could do the interview now so you don't have to rush over and that I'd run it by you two to fact check before I submit it and..." John paused mid-sentence. "Well... yes... the interview would have to be *on* the record. But I assure you that I'll let you see the draft and the revised..." Again he paused. "But it won't do me any good if it's not on the record. Then it's as though we never talked... but like I said, I promise that I'll..."

John grimaced, holding his phone to his ear and nodding as he listened. "Yeah. Right. I understand, but I promise that..." He winced and looked up at Jake who was busy writing on his napkin. "Yeah," he continued, his voice dropping in intensity. "I'm sure the interview will be worth the wait, but you can trust me to..." Again John went silent. "Okay, I understand. Sure. No problem." John paused, cocking his head like an animal listening to a high-pitched whistle. He then turned to Jake as a full grin erupted. "That would be great!" he exclaimed. "That would be amazing. Awesome!" He slapped the table with his open hand. "Yes! Sure. Not a problem. Whatever you say. We will be here." His smile still on high-beam, John disconnected the call and handed the phone to Jake.

"Did she promise you what I think she promised?" Jake asked, slipping the phone back in his pocket.

"Not only will this article run as a cover," John beamed, "she promised to set up an exclusive interview for me with Vinyl and guarantees that, too, will be a cover. Two covers!"

"That's it?" Jake picked up his bottle and took a drink.

"This could change everything. This is great. Amazing," John said in a near swoon. "I'm working on two covers. You're a writer. You get it."

"Yeah," Jake replied wearily, "I get it."

"She'll be here soon," John said reassuringly. "We can then do a quick interview and you can leave. This will be the best fucking article about you that's ever been written. It will have been worth the wait. I guarantee it. Plus, I'm getting these great personal Jake Jensen stories. I can never use them, but do you know how many people would pay to switch roles with me right now? I mean this is like sitting and listening to Hemingway, Mailer, Pynchon, Bukowski..."

"Do you practice being insulting? Jake grimaced. "You're not going to compare me to any of those in the article," he said pointedly. "If you are, this interview is over." He glowered at John, not a tinge of a smile on his lips.

"No," John cried. "It was meant to be a compliment. I don't know why I used Mailer. Some people like him."

"He wasn't the most offensive," Jake replied. He again checked his watch. Looking up at John, he asked, "You know the real difference between Millennials and Baby Boomers?"

John sat back, thrown by the sudden change in topic. "Age?" he finally offered.

"The difference is that forty-one percent of Millennials will buy a house sight unseen and only twelve percent of Baby Boomers will."

"How do you know?" John asked.

"A Redfin survey."

"You read real estate surveys?"

Jake grinned.

"And that's the difference?" John asked.

"Tells you all you need to know."

"Millennium-bashing time, right?" John asked, "It's a requirement nowadays—obsessed with social media, narcissistic, lazy, apathetic..."

"I like that. Keep going."

John grinned and took a drink. "Beating you to the punch. A learned protective response."

"Not all that concerned with them." He stopped, frowned, and then continued. "Only thing I don't understand is how you're all going on with your lives in such blissful obliviousness."

John shook his head. "Meaning?"

"Why aren't you in the streets? Rioting?" He picked up his napkin looking at the doodles he has made. "No matter," he said with a smile. "I'm just on the sidelines now. A watcher."

"But we are doing…"

"Let's change the subject," Jake interrupted. "So, staying in your neck of the woods, Sheila keeps preaching Instagram. She's infected and doesn't know it and like the smartest of plagues it masks its effect until it's too late."

"But she's right," John replied with a definitive nod. "Social media can do a lot of good. I just read where…"

Jake cut him off with a wave of his hand. "How about you write your questions on this napkin and I'll get back to you. Save us all time." He took his sunglasses out of his pocket. "Time for me to go."

"But she's on her way." John pleaded. "Tell me about…"

"Time's up," Jake said with a faint smile. "Time to get in bed, read, and fall asleep."

"Speaking of reading," John soldiered on, "you read Cheever?"

The waitress walked over. Jake looked up and shook his head. She nodded and left. "Do I read Cheever? Do *you* read Cheever?" he asked pointedly.

"Well, no, not really," John said apologetically. "But I read a review of one of your books and the writer compared you to Cheever. He said you were a bit of an anachronism. I believe 'an echo of another time' was the exact quote."

"I never read reviews, or Cheever."

"What do you think of Tom Wolfe's work?"

Jake looked away, an exasperated expression on his face.

John continued as though sloughing through swamp water. "What if I list writers and you either nod or shake your head? Okay, Vonnegut, Roth, Updike, Vidal, DeLillo, Pynchon..."

Jake released an intentionally loud sigh. "The white boy writers club?"

John responded with an embarrassed grimace. "I'm just saying that's where most reviewers place you."

"Stop talking about fucking reviewers," Jake snapped. "I made a deal with myself when I was twenty-three to only read writers who were dead—or born before 1920."

"Why 1920?"

"I like 1920. The Jazz Age, The Roaring Twenties, the Model T, prohibition... all the good stuff. Salinger just made the cut, 1919," he continued. "Henry Miller, 1891, was born before Fitzgerald, 1896 and Hemingway 1899? You wouldn't think that, would you? Virginia Woolf and Joyce, both 1882."

"You know when every writer was born?"

"Not after 1920." Carson McCullers made it. February 19, 1917. I have a crush on her, but that's between us."

John checked his phone while saying a silent prayer. "A text!" he exclaimed with a smile which faded as he read. "Sheila apologizes." He paused, staring at the phone as though hypnotized. He then continued, speaking slowly and deliberately. "She says we're going to have to reschedule. She asks if I can give you a ride home."

"Text her back and tell her she's fired," Jake declared.

"Not her fault," John said.

"Then tell her she's not fired."

John forced a smile. "In my experience whenever someone reschedules an interview, it never happens."

"I was going to interview Bowie," Jake said. "Before I arrived, he got into an argument with Peter Frampton. Turns out, Bowie threw a guitar against the wall and stormed out. There went my interview. Done. Gone. To this day it's swirling in rescheduling limbo."

"God, I'd hate to lose this," John said. "If this goes, chances are she won't follow through with the Vinyl interview. I'll lose both covers." He took a drink and ran his hands through his hair. He looked up at Jake. "Well," he said as though seeing his team had lost and conceding, "you're right. We should go."

"You go," Jake said, picking up his beer and finishing it. "Think I'll stay around here for a bit. Normally I'd go browse around the bookstore."

"Thought you wanted to go home and read."

"Jake smiled. "A pretext, a ploy, a ruse. Wanted out. Now school is over. I used to love just staring at books walking up the aisles, touching them, smelling them, taking my time. Hard to do now."

"You get accosted by your fans?" John asked. "Jake the rock star."

"Generally, just one or two nerd types, but that's all it takes. They latch on like leeches. You get to miss simple pleasures like browsing."

"Sheila asked me to drive you home. I should do that."

"You're off the clock now. Cheer up," Jake said, picking up John's beer and handing it to him. "If not this interview, another. Life is funny that way."

"You know how fucking hard it is to get a cover? You know how hard I've worked to...?" John stopped. He sighed and again he ran his hand through his hair. "Sorry," he said. "This meant a lot to me. This was going to..." his voice trailed off.

Jake picked up his pen and put it in his shirt pocket. He then stood up, took out his dark glasses and slid them on. He looked down at John. "I read in the Weekly that Sharon Stark is having a book signing at Book Soup. Apparently, this Sharon Stark person is tight with that sainted rock gal, St. Vincent. I remember hearing Sheila say that a buzz is building around Stark."

John tried to find Jake's eyes through the darkened lenses. He frowned. "Not sure I follow."

"Stark's star is on the rise," Jake said. "Her book signing was tonight. West Hollywood. Right around where Sheila seems to be. With the right rep, who knows where Stark could go. Could be the next Gummy Bears. A hurricane could be hurling her way."

"You don't think that Sheila...?" John shook his head. "You think she deliberately didn't... she wouldn't do that."

Jake grinned. "Don't know much about Stark, but I know she's young, hangs with rock stars, has a new novel. A perfect storm in the brewing."

"But Sheila wouldn't just..."

Jake took off his sunglasses, rubbed his eyes and slid them back on. "She probably thought she could swing both, be there with Stark and then get back here in time. Best laid plans..."

"But she wouldn't just leave you hanging."

"A miscalculation. Besides, I checked out a while ago. Side-stepping the hurricane was like getting off the ride at POP. I wouldn't get back on either. Sheila knows that." Jake took a step back and held out his hand. "Well..."

John stood and took Jake's hand and shook it. He forced a smile and looked towards the bar. "Probably won't be getting many more assignments at the magazine after this," he said, as though speaking to himself.

"You need a pen?" Jake asked pulling his pen out if his shirt pocket and holding it out.

"No," John said. "Always come prepared with pens."

"You might be able to use this one." Jake added, continuing to hold it up.

"No, really, I don't need..."

"Got this one on a site called Spy Guy. The best part of this pen is the voice-activated recording. Supposed to be able to record up to thirty-three hours of audio, but we didn't talk nearly that long."

John stared quizzically at the pen. "I'm not sure that I..."

"Everything we discussed is here," Jake replied, continuing to hold out the pen. "Take it as my Christmas gift."

John gingerly took the pen, continuing to stare at it.

"Protection," Jake explained. "I learned early-on to secretly tape my interviews. Comes in handy." He paused, removed his dark glasses and clinked them against the pen. "Our talk. What we discussed. All of it. It's recorded, documented." He paused again and added. "On the record."

"But Sheila...?" John asked, staring down at the pen as one would a precious stone.

"Is preoccupied."

"Jesus!" John exclaimed. He carefully put the pen in his pocket. "It will be a great piece," he promised. "The best. I guarantee you'll love it. I'll send you my draft. You can edit it however you..."

"Just write your article," Jake said. He looked around the room, picked up his beer and finished it. "Waste not, want not." He then slipped his sunglasses back on.

"Wearing sunglasses at night might not be the best way to remain inconspicuous," John said.

"It fools me," Jake replied. He paused and looked down. John could see himself reflected in the lenses as Jake smiled. "I've learned, that's what matters." He then turned and walked out into the Los Angeles night.

Ricochet
Autumn 1979

It was already dark when Jake Jensen exited the office of Triumph Advertising and climbed into his Mustang. It felt cold, probably in the 50s. Cold for L.A. He turned on the radio and hit the button for KRLA. "Bad Girls" by Donna Summer was playing. He quickly hit the preset for KFWB. "I Will Survive" by Gloria Gaynor had just started. He angrily punched the next button and "In the Navy" by the Village People filled the car, at which point he sighed dramatically, as though for someone else's benefit, and turned the radio off. 1979 was a bad year for someone who did not appreciate the finer points of disco. Jake drove east on Torrance Boulevard towards the 405 Freeway. It was a large street, an homage to concrete. A palm tree made a valiant stand every couple of blocks, but apart from that it was asphalt, sidewalks, and grey buildings. Leaving was the best part. That night, he had learned that his job would be over in two weeks—and then what? The most difficult part would be explaining it to Lana. She was ecstatic he'd landed the job at Triumph Advertising. His first grown-up job, as she defined it. From that starting point, she had enthusiastically charted Jake's life's trajectory. Triumph was the launch, he'd then get promoted, soon jump to a bigger agency and move up the ad ranks, ending up at a New York firm. There was no mention of his novel in her life plan. Jake was being groomed for success, not fantasy. After he accepted the position at Triumph, they had discussed him letting go of his apartment and moving in together. It was getting serious. And now Jake had to explain that he'd be jobless in two weeks.

It was a good night to use Jerry's key, Jake thought, as his Mustang crawled north on the 405. They needed a fun night together. He still had a job for two more weeks. Who knew what could change in two weeks? It was a night to celebrate. Dinner and then go to the house. His day hadn't gone as scripted, but he was closing in on his novel. That was his ticket. This was no time for glumness.

That night called for Jerry's key and the house. Jake's apartment wasn't an option. He liked its monk-like cloistered feel, but, at best, it could be described as a decent-sized closet. Lana's apartment was nice. Good sized. Airy. But they needed something different that night. They were just about living there as it was. It worked for Jake, since, between her job at Nordstrom's and law school, Lana was out most of the time offering him ample undisturbed time to write. Jake's apartment had become more of a waystation, a storage place, a place he kept his things. That night required something celebratory, something fun that could loosen the mood and pave the way for Jake to unveil his entrepreneurial plan. Presented correctly, Lana just might see the genius in it. It was a night for celebration—which called for Jerry's key.

Jerry, a quasi-friend and low-end drug dealer, had lent Jake the key before. Jerry's father owned rental property in Santa Monica. He leased furnished apartments and kept the power on while showing them, so they made for perfect getaways. Every now and then, when a house was vacant, Jake would cajole Jerry into lending him the key for a night. It was never an easy sell. It took quite a bit of badgering on Jake's part to wrest it from him. The last time Jerry repeated that his dad would kill him if he found out and emphatically stated that would be the last time he'd do it. He'd made that threat before, but this one seemed credible. So, in what Jake thought was a very clever move, he thanked Jerry, agreed to this being the final foray, took the key and immediately drove down to a hardware store to have a spare made. There was no need to continue bothering and worrying Jerry. The next day, Jake gave Jerry back his key, thanked him, kept the spare and figured what he didn't know wouldn't hurt him.

That particular evening called for the key. As Jake drove, he practiced his explanation of how he would soon be, once again, jobless. But there were huge upsides. He could now start his own company and would have time to write. Best of both worlds. His explanation would have to be carefully couched, spun, reframed. And best to break the news to her when they were relaxed. Jake stopped to pick up a bottle of wine and a bouquet of flowers. They'd have some fun at the house and then go out for a late dinner. He'd come up with a way to spin the story as a win for all. She'd understand.

Jake arrived at Lana's apartment, let himself in and announced that he was kidnapping her for the evening. It was Friday night, the weekend. Lana called out from the bedroom explaining that she'd had a rough day and was in need of kidnapping. Plus, she continued, they hadn't yet celebrated his landing the job at Triumph. They still had to toast, celebrate his new career. His new life. Dressed only in bra and panties, she leaned over and peeked out of the bedroom. Jake beamed holding out the wine and flowers, a double-fisted gift. She looked at him, smiled, an eyebrow arched. "A celebration? You already got a promotion!" she exclaimed.

"Something like that, only better," Jake replied. "But mum's the word until dinner."

"Come on," she pleaded. Jake shook his head. She then laughed, went over and kissed him. He held the gifts out as if preparing to fly.

Placing down the wine, he reached into his pocket, pulled out Jerry's key and held it up.

Lana looked at it and grinned. "Ah, a real celebration. Fun. But what are we celebrat...”?

“Come on,” Jake said. “We're wasting valuable seconds.”

They each then packed an overnight bag. Jake spent so much time at her place that everything he needed was there.

“Give me a sec to get dressed,” Lana said, grabbing some clothes and hurrying into the bathroom. Jake sat on the couch continuing to silently practice his explanation. Delivered correctly, she'd see it was the right decision on Jake's part.

Lana exited the bedroom wearing a low-cut, see-through, too-tight blouse showing ample cleavage, a skintight red mini skirt, shimmering stockings, and what she called her fuck-me pumps. She walked to the closet, picked up a video recorder and holding it high in her right hand announced, “Lights, camera, action!”

“Jesus!” Jake exclaimed, stepping back a few steps to take in the full impact of the visual.

“Don't bring him into it.” She turned seductively. “What do you think?” she asked, sashaying past Jake and parading through the bedroom. “Think I missed my calling?”

“You could be a very rich girl.”

“No kidding,” she said, dropping the video recorder on the bed and taking both of her breasts in her hands and jiggling them. “These girls could be money machines. Such a waste.”

Jake shook his head and laughed. “The legal profession's loss would be the sex industry's gain.” Standing, he grabbed his bag and the tape recorder. “Come on,” he said, heading towards the door. “Let's get over there, this is urgent!”

Lana smiled, struck a dramatic runway modeling pose. She then walked back towards the bathroom.

“What are you doing?” he asked. “Let's go.”

“I can't go outside dressed like this,” she said, looking down at her outfit.

"Come on," he insisted, "wear that when we go out tonight. It will be fun."

"Perfect if I run into someone from school. Everyone will think you're with a hooker."

"Lucky me," Jake said. "Besides, working a second job shows ambition, drive, determination." He looked up at her, held up the recorder and grinned. "I could be your agent, do your marketing, take thirty percent?"

"Five," Lana said playfully striking a seductive pose.

"Five? Twenty," Jake countered.

"Three," she shot back.

"Five in cash and fifteen in trade."

Lana paused and seductively walked up to him, "Two in cash and ten in trade."

"Done," Jake said, leaning in and kissing her, "but you drive a hard bargain."

"It's my job," she replied, playfully pulling away from him. "Plus, we didn't define my trade rate. You might have lost out big time." She laughed and headed towards the bathroom. "I am going to change," she said.

Jake sighed dramatically and sat back down. The excitement of Lana's visuals was being short-circuited by knowing he'd need to tell her about his exit from Triumph. He stood up and began to pace, silently rehearsing his explanation.

"Okay, let's go," she said, walking out wearing jeans and a form-fitting pink sweater blouse.

"Doesn't make that much difference," he said, picking up his bag and the video camera. "You're fuckable no matter what you wear."

"Fuckable?" she said, raising an eyebrow as she picked up her bag and walked to the front door. "Is that supposed to be a compliment?"

"The ultimate compliment," Jake replied. Fuckable was not the most sophisticated of terms, but apt, appropriate, accurate. Everyone wanted Lana. Jake sometimes wondered if he found Lana so desirable because others did.

They tossed the bags and video recorder into the back seat of Jake's car and headed to the empty house. It was in Brentwood, one of the east-west streets between Wilshire and San Vicente. It was a spacious house, well decorated. Jerry's dad leased furnished homes, so there were the basics—bed, sofa, chairs, dining room set, etc. He kept the electricity on between tenants to show it. It seemed lived-in, inviting. It was an ideal situation.

"We need to thank Jerry," Lana said as Jake pulled out the key and opened the front door. "I know he's nervous about his dad possibly finding out."

"Jerry's cool," Jake agreed. "A bit on the paranoid side, but cool."

"Speaking of paranoid," Lana announced, pulling a large joint from her purse and holding it up like a prize. "Ta da! It's the good stuff. Panama gold."

"It's huge," Jake said, taking the joint from her and inspecting it. "There's like a full lid wrapped in here. Where did you get it? That shit is expensive."

"Carla," Lana said with a slight shrug. "She always dates dealers and gets everything she wants for free." She paused pensively and then added, "Well, not exactly free."

Jake laughed and handed it back to her. "Carla is going to get herself in trouble one of these days."

"Going to?" Lana asked, picking up her bag and heading into the bedroom.

Jake followed. Placing his bag down on the bed and holding up the recorder, he turned towards Lana and grinned.

She smiled. "Before or after dinner?"

"You are dinner," Jake said, placing the camera back on the bed and unpacking.

"Lucky me. I guess I need to change then. I'll open the wine," she said, walking into the kitchen. "Jerry's dad really does make his rentals furnished," she called out. "There are glasses, utensils, dish towels, everything."

"Just heard from the director," Jake called out. "They're behind schedule. They need you on the set. Now!"

Walking back into the bedroom, Lana smiled, took out the joint, lit it and took a hit. "Tell that pervert director I'll make it worth the wait." She made her way over, kissed Jake and blew smoke into his mouth. She then handed him the joint.

"Just wine, tonight," he said shaking his head. Truth was the drug had turned on Jake. Instead of a fun pleasant high, he'd end up in high-alert paranoia. He felt cheated. For years what had been fun, relaxing, and sensual had overnight turned bad. Another relationship gone south.

They drank wine, Lana took a few more hits of the joint and put it out, saving it for a later date. They then cleaned up, making sure all traces of human life were erased from the kitchen. Jake walked to his overnight bag and returned with one of the plastic garbage bags he'd packed. "Everything has to be left pristine, exactly as it was when we entered," he said. "No trace."

Lana then walked over to a small TV set in the living room and turned it on. "Hey! It works!" she exclaimed. "Let's watch for a bit."

Jake shook his head. "No time. The director is really going to be angry if you make him wait any longer."

She grinned, sat up and headed towards the bedroom. She then picked up her skirt, top, and purse. "Going to prepare for my big scene," she said, walking towards the bathroom.

"Right," Jake said. Heading to the kitchen he poured them each more wine. He then went into the bedroom, placed the glasses on the nightstand, undressed, and picking up the video recorder, prepared to shoot.

The door opened and Lana emerged. Her hair had been teased, her makeup dramatic, her lips a wet ruby red. Her skirt and blouse clung to her like water. "You're naked," she exclaimed, staring at Jake in mock shock. "The director is naked!" Staring down, she added, "Naked and at attention."

"Combining method directing with method acting."

Lana laughed. "I forgot my script. Remind me what scene we're shooting."

"We are at a strip club," Jack began. "We came just to watch, but all of the guys there are looking at you instead of at the strippers. Their eyes are glued on you. They can't look away."

"Another day in the life," she said with mock sarcasm.

"They start teasing you," he continued, "saying you should be the one on stage. No one can take their eyes off you. You want them to watch. You take a few drinks, shyly climb onto the stage. You then start. "

"They all want me?"

"All of them."

"Want me so bad it almost hurts?

"Beyond almost."

Lana positioned herself in front of a full-length mirror on the bathroom door and adjusted her hair, making it look even more wild, tussled. "Who can blame them," she laughed, turning and striking a seductive pose. "Is there any music?" she asked. "A stripper needs music."

Jake looked around the room. "Hey, there's a stereo," he said, "Jerry's dad really knows how to show a place." The stereo was placed by the back wall of the bedroom. There were two small speakers placed on either side. To the right were albums standing in a small metal rack. "And albums!" he added. "We are in business." Jake walked over and, crouching down, began to search through the albums. "No, we're not," he corrected. "This is the worst."

"What do you mean?" she said. "What does he have? Pick something. Play something."

"I can't. This is the worst," Jake repeated. He read aloud as he thumbed through them, "'Le Freak'" by Chic, 'Do Ya Think I'm Sexy?' by Rod Stewart and 'Y.M.C.A.' by the Village People. The Bee Gees Greatest..."

"Okay, play that?"

"Are you crazy," he asked. "I can't play that. It will ruin the mood. That stuff is horrible. Jerry's dad must be fixated on disco. Ghastly stuff."

"Don't be such a fucking purist. Stop playing music critic and pick something."

"But I am a music critic," Jake insisted.

Lana glared at him. "Your actress is beginning to lose her inspiration."

"This is dreadful, dreadful stuff," he said with a shake of his head. "How can Jerry let his dad keep this stuff out? No one will rent this place when they see this."

"Those were all huge selling records," Lana said. "Now shut up and pick something."

"The late 60s gave us Woodstock and Hendrix, and what does 1979 give us? *Saturday Night Fever* and Andy Gibb," he said. "We are currently living in a pop culture nuclear waste site. Why doesn't he have an album by the Clash or..."

"Jake!" Lana snapped.

"No music," Jake said, continuing to shake his head, "because there is no music in this house. Nothing. Nada. You'll have to wing it. You're an actress, remember? You're on the set. Cameras are about to roll."

"Jake, put on something!" She then paused and, knowing there was no possible way he was going to place one of those albums on the turntable, she shrugged and said, "Okay no music. Right." Lana then closed her eyes and began to sway.

"Besides," Jake said standing up and walking away from the stereo, "it's not the music anyone's interested in."

"But they can't touch me," she said, continuing to move as she ran her hands over her breasts, down her stomach, between her thighs, "all they can do is watch."

"And they can barely hold themselves back. But you know that if you want them to touch you...."

"I just want them to watch... for now." She moved towards the edge of the room, struck a pose and began. Her body moved as she slid her blouse down first exposing one breast, then covering it, smiling, swaying and exposing it again. She removed her blouse and then slowly snaked out of her red miniskirt. Facing the wall, she dramatically turned towards the camera and teasingly removed her bra. Cupping her breasts, she held them up like prizes. She then turned around and, bending over, slid down her panties. Completely naked, she snaked onto the bed, placed a pillow under her head and spread her legs. Her body moved as she slid her hand between her thighs. Jake videotaped, moving closer to her, capturing her body's movements, her expressions. "You can barely stand it," he said. "One of them, the best looking one, the one you want is moving towards you."

Lana closed her eyes and began to softly moan. Jake had forgotten the tripod and hurriedly searched for a place to position the recorder so he could enter the scene. "Don't stop talking," she said.

"The one you want the most, can't hold himself back. He's watching every move you make, watching you touch yourself. He starts to unbutton his shirt as he moves towards you. You can feel him nearing as you feel the others watching, locked on your body. He's so close you can feel the heat of his body, but you keep your eyes closed." Jake placed the recorder on a chair, found the best angle possible to record and moved towards her. "You then feel a warmth between your legs, you feel his..." Jake abruptly stopped at the sound of footsteps followed by the sound of the front door opening. Lana sprang up, eyes wide, and stared at him.

"What was that?" she asked in a loud whisper.

Jake put his finger to his lips, motioning her to keep quiet. He then, as quietly as possible, turned off the recorder and moved towards his clothes. As he did so, he heard Lana scream, followed by another woman's scream. He turned just in time to see a woman rush out of the room. He looked at Lana, unsure of his next move. Before either of them could speak, she returned and, with wild eyes and open mouth, pointed a gun directly at Jake.

Jake raised his hands towards the ceiling. Lana stared in shock. The woman, who looked to be in her early thirties, was of middle height, auburn, dressed in black pants and a tailored, teal-colored, long-sleeved blouse. She looked more New York than L.A. At any other time, Jake would have found her attractive.

"Who are you?" she demanded. The gun swayed back and forth, her hand shaking as she pointed it from Jake to Lana then back again.

"Who are you?" she repeated in a staccato, scatter-gun, high-pitched voice. "What are you doing in my house?"

"But the house is empty. Nobody lives here," Jake replied, trying to make sense of the situation.

"I live here!" she screamed. "I fucking live here." She repeated the sentence as the gun waved back and forth. "What are you doing on my bed?" she said, looking at Lana. "Why are you in my house—naked?"

"We were... we were going to sleep," Jake explained. "We were tired." He stared down at Lana, whose eyes were on the gun, her mouth agape, as though locked in a silent scream.

"Sleep?" the woman demanded, pointing the gun towards Lana and then the video camera. "You're making a porn film in my house."

Lana silently nodded.

"No, no," Jake replied, moving to pick up his underwear, but thinking better of it and stopping. "We thought the home was vacant. No one has been living here and we... we found the key and..."

She turned the gun on Jake. "You *found* the key?" Before he could respond, she followed with, "Don't move!"

Jake watched as she edged to the doorway and looked into the other room where the phone was kept. It was an analogue world, pre-cell phones, a world where a phone had to be connected to a jack to make a call. Visibly shaking, the woman solidly planted her feet on the floor, took hold of the gun in both hands, and, as in a B-movie, continued to wave it between them. She took a deep breath and then said in an eerily calm voice, "I need you two to stand up and walk into the living room."

"Can I put on my clothes?" Jake asked.

The woman glared at him and motioned towards his clothes with the gun. "Your underwear. Make sure I see your hands at all times," she commanded. "I know how to use this."

Nodding repeatedly, Jake walked over to where his clothes lay in a pile on the floor, pulled his shorts on and started to pick up his pants.

"Just the underwear!" she snapped.

"But my jeans, I'm..."

"No!" she yelled. "How do I know what you have in your pants pockets. You're dressed enough for the police."

Jake stopped. "There's nothing in my pants pock..."

"This is how we're going to do this," she said, talking over Jake. "I'm going to move with my back towards the wall and you two are going to go single-file out through the bedroom door and into the living room to the phone. I will be following you with my gun trained on your heads. I can shoot this very quickly. Any sudden moves and..." she paused and then sharply asked, "you understand?"

"Just let us put our clothes on," Jake said. "We'll leave and you'll never see us again. No harm done."

"You call breaking and entering no harm? And I can smell the marijuana. You call drugs no harm? And porn!" she added pointedly.

"We thought the house was empty," Jake repeated. "It was an honest mistake. We'll go. We'll pay you. We'll pay you the same as if we rented a room for the night." Jake turned towards Lana who sat naked on the bed, staring at the gun.

The woman glowered at Jake and motioned towards the doorway with the gun. "Move slowly. Go!"

Jake nodded and began to edge towards the door.

The woman turned and pointed the gun at Lana. "You too," she commanded.

Lana looked up at her. She frowned and then raised an eyebrow.

"Get up and follow him," the woman commanded. "Single file. Slowly. This gun is trained on both of you."

"I'm naked," Lana replied.

"Nothing he hasn't seen before, and apparently not only him," the woman said, pointing the gun towards the video recorder. "Put your underwear on," the woman conceded. "Then slowly walk out to the living room."

Lana took a deep breath and bit her bottom lip. Jake could then see her body relax. "No," she replied.

"No?" The woman repeated, pointing the gun directly at her head. "What do you mean, 'no'?"

"No," Lana repeated in a calm even-mannered voice.

"You know that I'm in my rights to shoot you," the woman said. "You've broken into my home. You could be murderers, rapists. I'm protecting myself. I am in my rights. Get up!" she yelled so loudly that Jake jumped back and almost fell.

"I am not getting off this bed as long as you're pointing a gun at me." Lana explained. "Put it away!"

"Come on Lana," Jake said. "Don't make this any worse. Let's just do what she says."

"And you're probably not in your rights to shoot me," Lana added, sitting up straighter on the bed. "I'm in law school and I really don't think you are. I mean if you shoot me, a naked girl sitting on the bed, who is quite a few feet away from where you're standing, that's not going to look like any real threat. You're not in eminent danger, are you? I mean, we'll clearly be found in the wrong for being in this house, but at the very least you'll be charged with manslaughter. That will be a prison sentence. A long one. You'll be a felon for life and if you kill both of us, you'll most likely end up with life in prison, at the very least. We're clearly not armed. I'm naked. He's as good as naked. Neither of us have a criminal record and..."

"Shut up," The woman shouted. "You've broken into my home. I'd be perfectly in my rights. Get up and walk into that other room, or I am pulling this trigger. That is not a threat it's a prom…"

"Lana," Jake interrupted, trying to compose his voice, feeling as though he was trapped in a verbal tennis match in an insane asylum. "Come on. Let's go into the other room."

"And," Lana added jumping into full pre-lawyer mode, "if you shoot us while we're walking out, we'll have our backs to you. Shooting someone in the back never flies, well… unless you're a cop. Now that I think of it," Lana added, turning and looking at me, "We should both turn around. Face the wall. That way if she shoots us, we were not only naked and defenseless with no weapons, we had our backs to her. She'll end up locked up forever."

"Lana," Jake repeated, trying to sound composed. "This woman is quite agitated and is pointing a gun at us. Just get up and let's go into the other room. We can work everything out there."

Lana shook her head. She then turned, got onto her hands and knees and crawled to the head of the bed. There she stood up and facing the wall, put her legs apart and hands up against the wall as though ready to be searched. Jake found it an arousing visual, but poorly timed. "Shoot me and you're shooting a defenseless, naked woman in the back," Lana dared. "Either you let us put on our clothes and walk out of here, or I'm going to stand here and stare at your fucking blank wall."

The woman winced as though she'd been slapped. "You don't break into my house and give orders. Not while I'm the one holding the gun!" She moved towards Lana, her hands shaking more visibly as she pointed the gun at her. Slowly and loudly she commanded, "Get off my bed. Get up and walk into the other room or I'm shooting." She then yelled, "I'll fucking do it!"

A sense of panic shot through Jake. The woman was losing control. It would just take a minor squeeze of her finger to leave Lana bleeding, or worse, on the bed.

"If I kill her it's your fault!" the woman cried, turning the gun towards Jake for a second. She then took two more steps towards Lana, her hand quaking as she again targeted her. "Get off the fucking bed!" she yelled. "I will do it," she repeated, sliding into near hysterics. Her face was red, her eyes wide. The gun jerked up and down as though being pulled by an unseen magnet.

Lana remained silent, motionless and stood naked, her arms spread, hands against the wall. Neither seemed sane at that point, but the woman was passing from hysterics into something more dangerous. Jake took a deep breath and, not having a clue what he was doing, lunged at her. Like a defensive lineman trying to force a fumble, his left arm shot round her waist as his right hand grabbed for the gun. The two of them flew back and, as they fell, thudding loudly on the floor, the gun discharged with a deafening crack. The woman screamed as she fell, kicking at Jake wildly. His only thought was of the gun which slid and then came to rest a few feet away. He darted for it, grabbing it in his right hand and, pushing himself up, spun around and pointed it at the woman.

"Are you fucking crazy?" Lana yelled, glaring at Jake. She had fallen from a standing position and was crouched on the bed, her hands covering her head. "You could have killed me." Looking up and seeing that Jake was now the one holding the gun, she stood and glowered at him, hands firmly planted on her naked hips. Jake reflexively pointed the gun at her. "Are you crazy?" Lana repeated. "Don't point that damn thing at me. What the hell did you do? You could have killed me," she repeated.

"She was going to shoot you," Jake replied defensively. Jake had risked his life, done the whole knight-in-shining-armor routine, and she was yelling at him. Jake used the gun as a pointer, motioning it towards the chair. "You," he commanded turning towards the woman, who was now sitting on the floor, her head in her hands. "Go sit down on the chair."

"Don't point the gun at her." Lana commanded. "I hate guns. You hate guns. That is a very screwed up thing to do. Put that gun away!"

"She was about to kill you. I just saved your..." Jake stopped mid-sentence. He turned back towards the woman. "Go sit in that chair," he repeated, continuing to motion with the gun.

"What are you going to do to me?" the woman asked, slowly standing and making her way to the chair. "What are you, rapists? Murderers?" She stared at the video recorder and grimaced.

"We're not killing or raping anyone," Jake said in a near shout.

"You were raping her when I came in," she said pointing at Lana. "And you were taping it."

"I was not raping... I..."

"We were not..." Lana chimed in. She stopped and then started again. "Ok, I admit that we were about to fuck on your bed and if you want, we'd be more than happy to dry clean your bedspread. Although we just started, so I don't really think that..."

"Put your clothes on, get dressed, okay?" Jake said, pointing the gun towards Lana. "We need to get out of here."

"What the hell are you doing, Jake?" Lana cried. "I told you, do not point that gun at me!"

"No names!" Jake said in a loud impatient whisper, pointing the gun back at the woman. "Do not say my name! Come on get dressed."

"This is different," Lana said looking at the woman and cracking a smile. "He's never ordered me to put my clothes on before, it's usually..."

"Lana, please just get dressed," Jake pleaded. She had used Jake's name, which was disconcerting. Now, when the woman talked to the police, which Jake knew she would, she could say, the guy who broke into my house and pulled a gun on me was named Jake. Not that that would make any difference. The police would easily tie him back to Jerry and the key in record time. He began calculating how many years in prison he'd end up with and how old he'd be when he got out.

He turned towards the woman who was now sitting in the chair. "Look," he explained with as even-sounding a delivery as possible, "we've come here before when the house was empty and we thought it still was. We didn't know you were living here. An honest mistake. We're sorry. No harm done. We'll go. We'll pay you. I'm sorry."

"Jake, stop pointing the gun at her," Lana commanded, crawling back and sitting on the edge of the bed.

"Want to give her my last name, address, and social security number too?" Jake asked, pointing the gun at the floor.

"And," Lana added turning towards the woman, "why didn't you get the locks changed when you rented this place? That's the first thing you should have done." She shook her head and then continued as though admonishing a second grader. "That is very dangerous. You don't know who could have let themselves in. You're lucky it was us. Plus," she continued, her voice raising, "how were we supposed to know you were living here. It was almost like you set a trap for us. A lot of the fault falls on you, when you think of it."

The woman glared at Lana her expression shifting from fear to confusion to complete disdain. "You're both sick." She took a deep breath and stood up. "Let me go or I'm going to yell as loud as I can."

"A hell of a lot of good that will do," Lana said. "We've pretty much been yelling for quite a while and then shot off a gun to boot. I don't think your neighbors are exactly the responsive kind."

The woman turned towards Jake. "How did you get my key."

"It was a favor," he explained. "He was just helping me out and..."

"Mr. Tambor gave you the key to my house?" the woman asked. "That's illegal. Why would he give you the key when I live here?"

"No, not him," Jake quickly responded. "He wasn't involved. Look, it was an honest mistake, okay."

"Honest?" the woman replied.

"It was a mistake!" Jake repeated angrily. He paused. "It was my fault; I was lent the key a while ago. I made a copy of the key and gave him back the original, so technically, he didn't know that..."

"Who didn't know?" the woman demanded. "Who gave you the key to my..."

"You what?" Lana said, cutting the woman off. "You made a copy? Jerry doesn't know we're here?"

"No names!" Jake said adamantly. "I didn't want to keep bothering him," he explained. "I thought the house was still empty. But," he added, turning to the woman, "he didn't know."

"You made a copy and didn't tell me?" Lana demanded. "We could have been killed." She added, turning and glaring at the woman. "We almost were."

'Everything you've done is illegal!' The woman cried.

Jake simply stared from one to the other.

"Who is Jerry?" the woman demanded, acting as though she was still wielding the gun. "No one had the right to give you the key to my home."

"But he didn't know," Jake replied, "he had nothing to do with..."

"We didn't have permission to use it tonight?" Lana said, glaring at Jake as she picked up her clothes. "That is so fucked up."

"I made a mistake," Jake said with a shrug.

"No kidding. Look," Lana said turning to the woman, "we thought the house was empty. Who knew Jake was stupid enough make a copy of the key? That was so wrong," she added, turning towards Jake and glaring. "He fucked up, but we didn't know it had been rented. We'll leave, pay you for your bedcover and any damage the bullet caused and just put this behind us? We'll just forget this ever happened."

"Forget?" the woman repeated incredulously. She turned towards Jake and held out her hand. "Give me the gun."

Jake reflexively pointed it at her in response.

"Jake," Lana cried. "Do not point the gun at her. Put the gun down!"

Jake pointed it at the floor.

"You're going to keep my gun? That's burglary. And if you shoot me that's assault at best, murder at worst."

"I'm not going to shoot anyone and I'm not going to keep your gun," Jake said. "I hate guns and..."

"We're going and will leave it a block away," Lana interrupted. "We'll hide it in some bushes where you can find it after we go. We'll tell you exactly where we're going to put it. You shouldn't keep guns," she continued. "They're dangerous. They only have one purpose and that's..."

"Would you get dressed so we can go?" Jake said.

"Don't snap," Lana replied, as she began to put on her clothes. "Look," Lana continued, directing herself towards the woman and pointing to the corner of the wall. "The bullet went straight through. Just made a tiny hole. It will be easy to fix. Will look like new." She turned and glared at Jake. "That wall could have been me. That tiny hole there," she said, pointing again for emphasis, "that could be in my skull."

"She was about to pull the trigger," Jake replied, trying to keep from yelling. "I saved your goddamn life, okay?"

"We'll never know, will we?" Lana said. "Because you lunged at her setting the fucking gun off. So," she continued turning towards the woman, "we'll pay for the night and for fixing that hole and dry cleaning your bed cover. It will be as though this never happened. Deal?"

"Deal?" the woman seethed. "You tried to kill me."

"I grabbed the gun and it accidentally went off," Jake said. "You were pointing it at Lana. You were out of control. You were about to shoot her and…"

"Sure, broadcast my name," Lana said. She turned towards the woman. "You're fine," she continued, zipping up her jeans and buckling her belt. "He didn't attack you. He's right, you were out of control. But," she said, turning towards Jake as she put on her blouse, "You did tackle her. You gotta give her that. I mean you did lunge at her and land on top of her and you fired the fucking gun—at me!"

"I took it away from a woman who was about to blow your fucking head off!"

"Well, he's right there," Lana said, again turning towards the woman and shrugging as though begrudgingly yielding in a debate. "You were getting a bit on the manic side. You pretty much ruined our night and could have killed us. I think we're being damn civil here, considering we now have the gun, so why don't you…"

"We'll go," Jake said cutting Lana off. "I'll leave you the key. There are no others."

"Like I said," Lana added, "you should have changed the locks. That would have saved us all a lot of grief. I told you that you should have…"

"We'll pay for the locks as well," Jake jumped in.

Lana frowned. "I don't see why we need to pay for…"

Jake turned and glared, stopping her mid-sentence.

The woman sighed loudly, sitting and slumping back in the chair. "I just moved in and then—this! You've had the key the whole time.

Have you been slowly stealing from me all along? Spying on me? How often have you been here?"

"We don't steal. We haven't been here in over a month," Jake said. "You weren't living here then. We don't steal," he repeated. "We'll leave. Everything is okay."

The woman took a deep breath and looked up at Jake. "Okay? If you don't kill me, I'll probably end up in therapy forever."

"No one is killing anyone!" Jake exclaimed.

"I had a hard-enough time feeling safe as it was. Add this to the mix and…"

"But everything is okay," Lana said, with an open-faced everything's-fine smile. "Everything is fine," she continued, sitting on the bed and putting on her shoes. "We're not going to rape or kill you, we didn't steal anything, nothing's been damaged, except for that really small bullet hole which we'll fix—and we're going to pay you for your trouble. We're the good guys," she added, looking up at Jake and smiling. "It was an understandable mistake. We're sorry. Take this as an important life lesson. What you thought was a threat was nothing but a misunderstanding. You're here, you're safe, we're harmless and we'll take care of the inconvenience." Lana paused pensively and stared at the woman. "This is a great gift that we've just given you. Not many people get to experience something like this. Your boogie man has been reduced to a harmless kitten. And now, you'll love this place. You're in paradise and you're safe and we're just a couple who loves each other that made a silly mistake. This," she declared, "is a cosmic gift from us to you."

Silence followed. The woman stared at Jake, an expression of disbelief on her face.

"Where are you from?' Lana continued conversationally, trying to shift the dynamics of the situation.

"Where am I from?" the woman echoed, an incredulous expression on her face. "I'm going to make small talk with someone holding me hostage in my own home at gunpoint?" The woman closed her eyes and ran her hands over her face.

"Let's normalize this," Lana said. "Let's talk for a bit. Converse like rational human beings."

The woman sat up, folded her arms and looked straight ahead. She then turned towards Jake and spoke in a hushed tone. "I'm from Manhattan. I'm in publishing." She paused and glared at Lana. "Have we conversed enough? Can I have my gun now?"

"Publishing? How fucking cool is that?" Lana asked, turning to Jake with a broad grin. "This is fate. Kismet! Jake is a writer, and," she added after a dramatic pause, "he's looking for an agent or a publisher!"

The woman looked up at Jake, a scowl, on her face. "I'm sure he is."

"I'm serious," Lana persisted. "He's a writer. A real writer. He's had stories published. They're in literary journals no one has ever heard of, and he's never made any money doing it, but still... Plus, he now works at an advertising agency. Paid to write... finally. He's an account executive at... what's the name of the agency?" she asked, turning towards Jake.

"Why not just give her my resume and draw her a map to my place?" Jake asked.

"Lighten up, Jake," Lana said with a frown. "What difference does it make? It's going to be easy enough for her to find us if that's what she wants to do. We need to move from an adversarial position to one of cooperation, with this whole writing thing, maybe collaboration, who knows, even friendship."

The two of them silently started at Lana.

"So, Lana continued, "like I was saying, Jake works for an advertising firm called..." she turned to Jake.

"I really don't think where I work is going to be of any interest."

"Jake!" Lana said impatiently.

Jake paused and then slowly pronounced, "I don't really work there anymore." He wasn't sure why he offered that information then. That wasn't the plan. He had been trying to find the right time, the best way to comfortably bring that up, but with all of the confusion... perhaps he realized that there never would never be a right time, so he just blurted it out. "I'm only there for two more weeks."

Lana frowned looking from Jake to the woman and back again. "What do you mean?"

Jake shrugged and looked down at the gun. "Long story. Tell you later."

"Make it a short story. And tell me now," Lana said tersely. "What the hell happened? You just started this job." She turned to the woman and repeated, "He just started..."

"I don't care!" the woman cried. With that she began to stand up.

"Sit down. Don't move," Jake demanded, again pointing the gun at her.

"You're not going to shoot. No one here has the guts to pull the trigger." The woman stood and headed into the living room.

"Sit down," Jake repeated weakly. He turned to Lana who shot up off the bed, and raced past the woman into the living room. Grabbing the phone, she unplugged the receiver's cord, rendering it useless. "Let's talk about this like civil human beings," Lana said holding the receiver behind her back. "We don't need guns or the police. We just need to talk things through."

The woman, an expression of disbelief on her face, stared down at the now useless phone and then back at Lana. "Give that to me," she demanded, holding out her hand. "You've ruined my phone."

"It's not ruined," Lana explained. "As soon as the cord is plugged back in it will work good as new."

The woman looked back towards Jake as he entered the room. She stared down at the gun, took a deep audible breath and headed for the front door.

"Where are you going?" Lana cried, rushing past the woman and planting herself in front of the door, blocking the woman's exit. The woman stopped a foot away from Lana, who was the larger and seemingly stronger of the two. They silently glared at one another.

"Move aside and let me walk out of my house," the woman demanded.

"You can go," Lana said. "But just not yet," she quickly added. "Let's talk, okay? Let's just talk. We'll take care of everything, we'll leave, you'll calm down and all will be good as new."

The woman stood so close to Lana they were almost touching. "Get out of my fucking way!" she commanded.

Lana turned towards Jake, a perplexed, questioning expression on her face.

"Wait," Jake called out. "Look," he said, holding up the gun. He opened the cartridge, removed the bullets, closed it and walking over to the woman, held it out. "Here," he said, handing it to her.

"Are you crazy?" Lana snapped.

"There are no bullets," Jake replied, "besides, it's hers."

The woman hesitantly reached out and took it. "Now the bullets," she said looking up at Jake.

"I have money in my wallet," Jake said, ignoring her request and pointing towards his pants in the bedroom. "If I don't have enough to cover everything, I'll get more. I'll cover everything."

The woman glared at the bullets in his hand.

"You'll cover everything?" Lana asked sarcastically. "With what money? You quit your fucking job, remember?"

"I'll cover it," Jake repeated, ignoring Lana. "I lied to Jerry. He didn't know I made a copy of the key. None of this is his fault. I'll take care of it."

"Who is Jerry?" the woman replied, continuing to glare at Jake's hand. "The bullets."

"Don't mention Jerry," Lana barked, looking at Jake with an expression of total exasperation.

"You're the one who said it doesn't matter what she knows," Jake said angrily. "He was just being a good guy, helping a friend out," he continued, turning back towards the woman. "What can we do to make it okay?"

The woman turned back towards Lana who stood sentry in front of the door. "Move out of the way."

"Besides that," Lana replied.

The woman turned, walked towards a bureau.

"What are you doing?" Lana said. "What is she doing?" she repeated turning to Jake.

The woman opened the drawer and pulled out a box of bullets. Placing the box on the table, she calmly opened the gun cartridge and taking the bullets out of the box, began to load.

"Are you crazy?" Lana said. "Is she crazy?" she repeated turning towards Jake. "Stop her!" Seeing that he was simply standing and watching, Lana rushed towards the woman, tossed the phone receiver on to the couch and ripped the box off the table, causing bullets to fall and roll over the floor. She then grabbed and pulled the gun out of the woman's hand. "No more guns. No more bullets. No more shooting. Why didn't you stop her?" Lana cried turning towards Jake, holding the gun up as if in evidence. "Stand in front of the door," she said impatiently.

Jake shrugged and did as directed. Lana marched into the bedroom, hurriedly finished dressing, walked back into the living room and stood next to Jake in front of the door. "I'll see she doesn't leave," she directed. "Go get dressed, grab your bag and the recorder and let's get the fuck out of here."

"But we can't just leave," Jake said. "I mean we need to figure out…" He paused and met Lana's frozen stare. He then shrugged, headed into the bedroom, hurriedly dressed, put the bullets in his pants pocket and walked back into the living room carrying his bag and video recorder. The woman was sitting on the couch when he returned. She looked up at Jake and grimaced.

"It was a mistake," Jake said again "I'll pay you for…"

"Let's get out of here," Lana interrupted. "She's crazy." She paused and glared at Jake. "You're both crazy. You quit your fucking job? After two weeks? I don't believe it. No, I take that back. I do. That is so you. What are you going to do now? Write more stories that nobody reads or pays you for? Is that plan B Jake? 'Cause you're not coming back and living off of me, got it? Not anymore. I can't believe you already quit," she said with a shake of her head.

"I did not quit," Jake pronounced.

"Oh great, you were fired in less than a month. That's worse."

"I was not fired!" Jake said adamantly. "Look, I was going to tell you later," he began, glancing at the woman and then back at Lana. "This was supposed to be a celebration." Seeing the impatience and disbelief in Lana's expression, he began to speak more quickly, the words accelerating as he went. "James and I are starting a company in two months. I was going to give notice then. But today Kartoff, my boss," he said, glancing down at the woman," told me he was giving me a promotion and a raise, but in order to do that they were going to fire Dan, the other copywriter. I didn't want Dan to lose his job, so I told him that I'd give my notice today, if he'd tell Kartoff that he couldn't start for two months, that way I'd keep my job until James and I start the company, Dan wouldn't lose his job and the company would still have a copywriter. Dan said okay, but then he lied. I gave my notice and he didn't say anything. He just stood there. So Kartoff offered him the promotion and the raise and I was given my two-week notice. But that wasn't the plan," he ended breathlessly. "That's not what we agreed on."

Lana glared at Jake. "That's the dumbest story I ever heard," she said. "A promotion and raise? And you quit?" She turned to the woman and pronounced, "He quit." Turning back to Jake, she raised her hand as if pleading. "What the fuck were you thinking?"

"Can we discuss this later?" Jake asked.

"Nothing to discuss." Lana turned and stared pensively at the woman. "If we leave and she calls the police we'll be traced in minutes. Sitting ducks. "We can't just... We need time. Maybe we should tie her up," Lana said looking towards the bedroom. "At least that will buy us a little time, before she does whatever lunacy she's going to do."

"Tie her up?" Jake asked. "Are you crazy? This was an honest mistake, that would be..."

"Promise you won't call the police," Lana said, staring down at the woman. "Give us your word and we won't tie you up."

The woman silently looked up at Lana. She then stood up and started heading for the door, moving like a zombie in a low budget film.

"What are you doing?" Lana cried, rushing towards the door and pointing the gun at her. She positioned herself between the door and the woman. "I told you," Lana said turning towards Jake. "She's crazy." She looked back towards the bedroom. "Maybe she has some cord, or we can use the sheets, or nylons—those work. Where do you keep your nylons?" she asked, turning towards the woman.

"We're not tying her up," Jake said. "What is wrong with you?"

"What's wrong with me?" Lana replied, waving the gun in Jake's direction. "Am I the one who quit my job? Am I the one who fucking made a copy of the key and had us break into someone's home? Was that me?" She paused and pointed the gun at the woman, "If I could believe you wouldn't call the police, we could call this a night—a really fucked-up night."

The woman stared at Lana. "Move out of my way," she said.

"You're fucking nuts, you know that?" Lana said. "Go sit down." The woman stood in place and stared at Lana. "Now!" she commanded, holding the gun out. The woman continued to stare, she then turned and walked to the chair opposite the couch and sat.

Lana pointed the gun at Jake. "Give me the car keys."

"Don't point the gun at me!" Jake said. "You're the one who said you hated guns."

"Give me the key," she repeated.

"She wants to tie me up," the woman said turning towards at Jake. "Then she's going to shoot me."

"No one is going to tie you up," Jake said with a shake of his head. "Lana is a bit overwrought. It's making her say nonsensical things."

"Give me the fucking car key!" Lana repeated.

"We can't just leave," Jake replied.

Lana looked from Jake to the woman. "Really? Watch. The key!"

Jake reached into his pocket, took out his keys, removed the car key from the ring walked over and handed it to her.

Lana put the key in her pocket, placed her hand on the doorknob and turned it. "Thanks for a great night, Jake. Look at the position you put us in." She turned the knob and opened the door. "We're fucked.

And he quit his job," she said looking at the woman.

"I didn't just quit," Jake said. "It's part of a plan. I was going to explain it to you. It's going to be okay. I have another offer and..."

"As long as we're all sharing," Lana said, cutting Jake off mid-sentence. She paused, looked at the woman, turned back towards Jake and pronounced, "I slept with Jerry."

Jake swayed backwards, feeling as though he'd been physically hit. He started from the woman back to Lana, opened his mouth to respond, but said nothing.

"Thanks for sharing. Can I have my gun back?" the woman said, turning to Lana and holding out her hand.

"But you said he was geekish," Jake said accusingly, "how could you possibly sleep with...?"

"Fucking grow up!" Lana snapped.

Jake reached into his pocket, took out the rest of the bullets and walked towards the woman. "Here," he said, handing them to her.

"Thank you," she said. "Can I now have the gun?"

"What are you doing?" Lana said. "You suddenly switching teams because your feelings have been bruised? What good are the bullets going to do her if I have the gun?" Lana again pointed the gun at the woman. She paused, pensively bit her bottom lip, turned towards the bedroom and smiled. "It just hit me. Our problem is solved."

"I don't have a clue what you're talking about," Jake said. He then walked over to the couch and sat down. Finding the phone receiver lodged between the couch cushions, he picked it up and held it out to the woman.

"Thank you," the woman said. She stood and, walking over, took the receiver from Jake. She then headed over to the phone, plugged in the receiver.

"What are you doing?" Lana said, pointing the gun at the woman.

"Have you both gone crazy?" she added, turning and pointing the gun at Jake.

"I'm calling the police," the woman explained. "You broke into my home, attacked me, shot at me, and are holding me hostage."

"Put the phone down!" Lana ordered.

The woman picked up the receiver and began to dial.

"Grab the phone from her," Lana commanded. "Jake! Grab the fucking phone!"

Jake motionlessly watched as the woman dialed.

"Jesus Christ!" Lana yelled. Then holding the gun in both hands like in a TV western, she aimed towards the body of the phone, grimaced and fired. The woman screamed and jumped back as the phone flew out of her hand, landing against the wall.

"Good work, Lana," Jake said sarcastically. He then turned towards the woman, "We'll pay you for the phone."

"She shot me," the woman cried, staring at the phone lying on the floor. "She tried to kill me."

"God that's loud," Lana said proudly as she stared at the gun. "I didn't know it kicked that way. I almost went flying backwards." She then looked at the woman and continued. "I did not try to kill you and I did not shoot at you. I shot at the phone and the only reason I did that was that Jake Jensen here was too busy sulking to grab it from you. Blame it on him." She turned towards Jake. "Are you over your sulk? Can we wrap up here now?"

Jake shrugged.

"Sit down and we will figure this out and be out of your life forever," Lana said pointing the gun at the woman. "Like Jake said, we will pay for any damage. Well, more aptly, I will, because Jake here no longer has a job."

The woman slowly walked to the couch and sat down.

"Good," Lana said. "I appreciate that. So, if we need it, this is going to be our story—it was basically a double date, Jake and I and you and Jerry. We had some drinks, smoked some weed, were getting ready to shoot a video starring the four of us and then things turned ugly."

The woman stared at Jake, a perplexed expression on her face.

"You," Lana said, pointing the gun at the woman, "found out that Jerry and I had slept together. Jake went into the corner to sulk, but you were fuming, mad as hell that Jerry, your boyfriend, had cheated on you."

"Who is Jerry? The woman asked, staring at Jake with a look of disbelief.

"It was all too much for you," Lana continued. "You stormed to the bureau and grabbed the gun you keep there," Lana paused, bit her bottom lip and then went on. "You came back into the bedroom and pointed the gun at Jerry. You were losing control. I tried to take it from you but in the scuffle, we fell and it discharged. That explains the bullet hole in your room."

"Hey," Jake protested, "I was the one who..."

Lana frowned and continued. "Then, seeing you had completely lost control, I ran to the phone in an effort to dial the police but you scrambled for the gun and shot the phone out of my hand. Jerry got behind you and ripped the gun out of your hand..."

Jake shook his head. "I was the one who took the gun..."

"Jerry then panicked," Lana continued, "grabbed his stuff, handed me the gun and ran out, leaving just the three of us to work things out. You're good to be rid of him," she added with a grin. "In time, I was able to assure you both that the incident with Jerry was a one-night stand and..."

"Was it?" Jake asked.

"Just one of those things that happens," Lana forged on, "and that it would never happen again. Eventually, using my negotiation skills, the situation was resolved and Jake and I left."

"Who is going to believe that?" the woman asked.

"Anyone," Lana replied with a smile. "Everyone." She paused and added. "But, if you are crazy enough to call the police, there is an epilogue—after we left, you continued drinking alone, you whipped yourself up into a frenzy, livid that Jerry had betrayed you. You wanted revenge, so you called the police and made up this insane, nonsensical lie about us breaking into your house."

Jake shook his head. "Jerry will never agree to that. He won't want to be implicated. He'll say that..."

"But he already is," Lana replied with an impatient sighed. "Implicated. He was the moment he handed you the key. In my story, he's confessing to having sex with two women. Two rather attractive women, I might add. What guy is going to have an issue confessing to that? In her story he has illegally given you the key to her home, leaving him and his father legally responsible for whatever happened while we were here. We're talking steep fines, possible jail time for both Jerry and his father. Which version do you think he'll go for?"

"How would he even know her?" Jake asked, turning towards the woman.

Lana shrugged. "Who knows. Who cares? He was walking by a property that his father owns, saw an attractive woman and took advantage of the situation to introduce himself. That's possible. He asked her out, they dated. He introduced her to us and they invited us here for an evening that went very very wrong."

"Yeah," Jake protested, "but what if Jerry..."

"I'll take care of Jerry!" Lana snapped. She turned towards the woman. "Or I don't have to make up any of this silly story. We can pay you for your time and trouble, leave and all go on with our lives. That's up to you."

The woman silently glowered at Lana.

Lana nodded as if in agreement with a statement. "Well, in that case, we'll need a bit more insurance." She turned towards Jake. "Stand in front of the door," she said, motioning towards the door with the gun.

Immobile, Jake stared at her.

"Jake, please," Lana said. "Just for a minute. I need to get our things."

Begrudgingly, he walked over and stood in front of the door.

"Thank you," Lana said. She then walked into the bedroom. "This will just take a minute," she called out. "Make sure she stays where she is."

The woman stared at Jake and then looked at the floor, a vacant expression on her face. He stared at the phone lying on the floor, a bullet hole in the middle of the casing.

"I'm sorry," Jake said. "I didn't know that... we'll take care of everything." His voice trailed off. The woman stared down at the floor and they remained silently in place until Lana returned.

"Well, look what I found," Lana announced, entering the room and looking down at the woman. She held up a baggie filled with marijuana. "See, we do have something in common."

The woman looked up at the baggie.

"Don't worry, I'll put it back," Lana continued, "with a gift. Well plural," she corrected herself, "gifts. I stashed some joints and Quaaludes in various places around your bedroom. Like I said—gifts. You might find some of them, but I doubt you'll find them all. If the police are called in and you drag us into this, not only will Jerry confirm my version of the story, I'll make sure the officers of the law are somehow directed to your stash."

"Quaaludes?" Jake said. "More joints?"

"That Carla," Lana replied sarcastically. "So, if you do decide to call the police, it won't look good for any of us, but it will be written off as some kind of silly domestic squabble that police find themselves dealing with every day. You'll be seen as complicit as any of us. More, actually, because it took place in your home. And then, when they find the drugs... well you can only imagine. Those will point only to you, possession being nine-tenths of the law and all that."

The woman glared at Lana. "You're sick," she said. "You're a monster."

Lana smiled. "A lawyer. Well, almost a lawyer. A problem solver and I'd say I've pretty well solved this problem." She turned towards me. "I'll leave your car parked in front of my apartment. How you get there is your problem. The keys will be under the mat. Don't bother coming up." She turned towards the woman and smiled. "We'll pay... well I'll pay for... whatever. I'll throw in the locks. Get an itemized bill. You can give it to Jake." With that, Lana walked to the door and opened it. "Whoops, almost forgot," she said, staring down at the gun in her hand. "There is a snugness to this you know" she said. "It's almost comforting. Who knew?" She then walked to where the woman was sitting, opened the gun cartridge, emptied the bullets and dropped the gun on the couch next to her. "I'll save these as a memento," she said, sticking the bullets in her pocket. With that she turned and walked out.

The woman stared at Jake pensively, she then picked up the gun, walked over to the bureau, picked up the box of bullets and methodically began to load. "Today was the first time I ever fired this thing," she said. "It's much louder than I would have thought."

Jake nodded.

She walked over to the phone and, picking it up, put the receiver to her ear. "It still works," she said. "Your girlfriend is sick," she added with a frown. "Certifiable. How do you stand her?"

"I doubt she's my girlfriend any longer," Jake replied.

"Lucky you. You two do that often?" she asked, motioning to the bedroom, "that whole video recorder porn bit."

Jake looked towards the bedroom, wistfully thinking that those days were over. "I really thought this place was vacant," he said. He had uttered that phrase so many times in the last few hours it was almost automatic. A catch-all sentence, a mantra. He walked to the chair opposite the couch, dropped down and ran both hands over his hair. "This has been a horrible day," he said. "I gave away my job, my relationship is over, Jerry will never talk to me again, his father will probably sue me, and you're going to turn me into the police. I'll be a felon from this day on." He paused and then continued. "There are also drugs here somewhere, so you might as well throw drug possession, or better yet, possession for sale into the mix."

"And don't forget that your girlfriend had sex with Jerry," the woman added.

He nodded. "Thanks."

The woman stared at Jake. "It's not as though my day has been great," she said. "I got lost on the freeway on my way home. I hate these freeways. Then came home to find out my home had been broken into and a porn film was being shot in my bedroom, I was physically attacked and shot at twice, and there have been drugs planted somewhere in my home. I'm starting a new job tomorrow and I'm going to be a nervous wreck. So, don't sit there feeling sorry for yourself."

Jake nodded and they sat in silence. The woman picked up the gun and began pointing it at various objects around the room, as though she was going to shoot it. She then pointed the gun at Jake and yelled,

"Bang!" pretending as though the gun was recoiling in her hand.

"Hey," he said, flinching away from the gun, "that's not funny. That's not a toy."

The woman looked down at the gun, but kept it pointed at him. "Didn't do me all that much good," she said. "You two could have raped me, killed me. Didn't really help." She looked up at Jake. "You terrified me, you know."

Jake nodded and looked away. "I'm sorry," he muttered.

The gun suddenly discharged, the bullet flying to the left of Jake. Terrified, he yelled and dropped to the floor. "What the fuck!" he exclaimed. "What did you do? You shot at me. You could have killed me."

The woman stared at the gun and grinned. "Only if I was a really really bad shot, which I guess I could be since I have no idea how to use this. I was aiming away, not at you. Seems only fair I get a shot. You shot the gun in the bedroom. The lawyer slut shot at me here. Seemed right I have a turn."

He pulled himself up, starting to sit, but thinking better of it, remained standing. "But you fucking shot at me," he repeated.

"So now we're even," she replied, "well, somewhat even. I didn't invade your home."

"But you shot…"

"An intruder? A thief? A burglar? A rapist? A murderer? Who knows?"

"Come on, I gave you your gun, your phone, you really think I'd do that if I was a criminal?"

She shrugged. "I figure there are all sorts of criminals. And considering the situation, that thought's not that big a leap."

"Well don't do that again."

She paused and looked up at Jake. "Your girlfriend is crazy. You know that, right?"

"It's been a bad day for her too," he said defensively. "You didn't get her at her best."

"Best?" the woman replied with a mock laugh. "You with her because she looks good? Good in bed? Lets you take sex videos?"

"No. I mean, yeah, she's gorgeous and..."

"She is not gorgeous," The woman corrected. "Attractive at best, in a slutty porn star sort of way—running around naked, tits bouncing up and down." The woman paused and then declared, "Your girlfriend is a slut."

"I know I've ruined your night," Jake said, "but that's no reason to start calling Lana a..."

"She'd be a slut whether you ruined my night or not," the woman continued. "She slept with Jerry, whoever he is, and we both know he's not the only one—not by a longshot." She stopped and then emphatically pronounced, "A slut!"

"I'm not discussing Lana with you," Jake said. "She's great. She's fun and..."

"You're big on fun," the woman said, staring down at the gun and frowning. "Must be an L.A. thing."

"Can you please put that down?" Jake asked, staring at the gun in her hand. "Can't I just pay you for... whatever? I can then leave and we'll forget this ever happened?"

"Forget?" the woman exclaimed, pointing the gun at Jake. She motioned towards the chair. "Sit down," she directed, "you're making me nervous." She paused and then added, "You're lucky to be rid of her."

"Yeah," Jake said, sitting down, "today is my lucky day." He motioned towards the phone. "If you're going to do this, let's get it over with. Make the call."

"Why don't you just do what your slut of a girlfriend did?" the woman asked, as she placed the gun down and picked up the phone. "Get up and go. Chances are I won't shoot you."

"Go where?" He pointed towards the gun lying on the couch next to her and added, "What you're doing right now is not smart."

She looked up at him, a questioning expression on her face.

"Putting down the gun to pick up the phone is not a good idea," he continued. "If I really was a criminal, I'd take this chance to lunge for the gun. You wouldn't have a chance."

The woman looked down at the gun but did not move to pick it up. She then placed the phone down on her lap, replaced the receiver and stared at Jake. "You think they'd convict me if I shot you? Wouldn't I be in my rights, you being a burglar and all. Don't you think I'd get off?" She paused and smiling added, "I could always hire your ex-girlfriend to defend me."

He stared at her and after a long pause said, "That slut?"

The woman laughed. "You're funny."

"I'm a riot," Jake said. "Particularly with a gun pointed at me. What are you doing with a gun anyway? None of the women I know own guns."

"They're all busy shooting porn videos," she said.

"I'm serious," he said, "I don't know anyone who owns a gun. Well, except for this one drug dealer friend."

"With friends like yours," she paused and then added, "it was a gift. From a friend."

"Some gift. Some friend."

"A good friend," she snapped angrily. "He figured I'd need it moving to L.A."

"You'd need that a heck of a lot more in New York than L.A."

"Yeah? Was my home ever broken into in New York? Was I ever shot at in New York? Was I ever...'?

"Okay, okay... Point taken." he replied. "But still, it was all a mistake."

The woman looked back at the gun. "But, like I said, it didn't help much." She got up and walked into her bedroom. "You'll pay to replace the bullet hole damage?" she called out. "You'll replace the locks and..."

"Anything," Jake jumped in. He stared towards the bedroom, his eyes widening. "You name it. I'll pay for anything you want."

The woman walked back into the living room, and nodded. She picked up the phone and placed it on the bureau. "I don't think this move to L.A. was the best decision I ever made," she said. "I'm tired," she added. "I'm really really tired."

Jake nodded. He looked towards the door and then turned back to her. "You hungry?" he hesitantly asked.

The woman frowned. "Am I hungry?"

"I haven't eaten," he said with a slight shrug, "I thought that maybe if you're hungry that..." he paused.

She looked at the gun, but more as a curiosity than a weapon. "You're asking me to dinner?"

"No," he replied hurriedly, hearing how strange that sounded. "I just mean if you're hungry, there's Zucky's on Wilshire at Fifth. It's a deli. It's open 24 hours. It's late and if you're hungry..." he stopped, looked down, and shook his head.

The woman, still holding the gun, stood up and walked back into the bedroom. "The bullet hole is small," she said talking loud enough for Jake to hear her in the other room. "Shouldn't cost much to repair." She walked back into the living room and placed the gun on the bureau. She then picked up the phone receiver and put it to her ear. "It still works, but it's ruined. I'll need a new one."

"Yes, sure. Definitely," he said.

"And I'll need new sheets and a bedcover now that..."

"But we never..." he stopped mid-sentence. "Yeah. Sure," he agreed.

"You make a lot of these?" she asked, looking down at the video recorder.

Jake shrugged. "We make them sometimes. Or I guess *made* them sometimes is more accurate. Anything to do with Lana is past tense at this point."

The woman picked up the recorder and studied it. "How much do you sell them for?"

"We don't sell them," he said defensively. "They're not porn. They're just for us. You know, fun."

"Fun again," the woman replied. "Yeah, she seems to be big on fun." She paused as she carefully studied the recorder. "What else do you think she lied to you about?" she asked looking up at Jake. "Maybe *she* sells them."

"Of course she doesn't sell..."

"They could be in porn stores all around the country for all you know. Or maybe she just shares them with her friends, you know, for fun."

Jake sat down on the chair opposite the couch, and stared blankly at the floor, trying to figure out how the night had gone so incredibly wrong. "I lied to her too," he said. "Didn't tell her about the key, about my job."

The woman shrugged, walked over to the bureau. "She was the one who worried me," she said as she opened the drawer, put in the gun and locked it. "A loose cannon—but fun."

"Are you going to call?" Jake asked looking over at the phone.

"Wouldn't do me much good would it? Your girlfriend will tell the police that made-up story. She'd do that right?"

"Not maliciously," Jake said. "I mean she wouldn't do that to hurt you, but to protect us. Only if you called the police and forced her to."

The woman laughed. "So now I'm the one who's attacking that poor innocent slut."

"I didn't mean... and would you please stop calling her a..."

"She'll paint me as a part of a sick foursome who makes disgusting porn films with some creep named Jerry that I've never met, who is apparently a total slime who sleeps with his friend's slutty girlfriend. I also apparently tried to shoot her with my gun. Not to mention the fact that I have a variety of drugs I don't know about stashed throughout my place. No—don't think calling the police is the best idea." She walked towards Jake and held out her hand. "How about I keep the key?"

Jake nodded, reached into his pocket and, pulling the key out, dropped it in her hand.

"Any other copies?"

Jake shook his head. "Just made the one."

"Honestly?"

"Just made one. I'm sorry," he said.

"Me too," she said, putting the key in her pocket. "More than sorry."

Jake nodded and ran his hands through his hair "You really in publishing?"

"You really a writer?" she replied, walking towards the front door.

Jake shrugged. "I write. Lana would probably say I'm not. More a wannabe, or a fuck up."

The woman opened the front door and looked out. She then looked back at Jake. "To answer your question, I am hungry," she said.

Jake began to respond, but was unsure whether she was simply stating the fact that she was hungry or saying she'd like to go with him to get something to eat.

"Here's the deal," she continued, "you pay for the damage and for my dinner and I won't..." she paused, "and we're even."

"You serious?"

"I don't lie."

Jake took a deep breath, exhaled and stood up. "That is the best offer I've ever had," he smiled.

"Ever?" she asked.

"Considering everything, yeah, by a long shot." He paused and then said, "There's something I need to ask."

"What?" she replied, looking at him suspiciously.

"Those albums," he said, looking towards the bedroom, "they're not yours, are they?"

"They're not?" she replied.

"Well what I mean is, you don't really listen to them."

"I don't?"

"Well no," he replied. "I mean you don't seriously listen to the Village People."

She smiled, struck a mock singing pose, held her hand to her mouth as though she were grasping a microphone and belted: "It's fun to stay at the YMCA. It's fun to stay at the YMCA." She laughed. "They're fun," she said, "you like fun."

"Fun, not lunacy. I should have shot them when I had the gun," he said, glancing back towards the bedroom, "There wasn't one album we could use when..." he stopped mid-sentence.

"If I'd known you were going to break into my home to shoot a porn film, I would have been more selective," she replied.

He shook his head, placed his hands in his pocket and pulled out his keys. "Shit, I don't have my car," he said staring down at my keyring. "She took it."

"She seems good at that," the woman said. "Taking things." The woman walked into the bedroom. She came back carrying her purse. Opening it, she held out her keys. "I'll drive. You pay for the gas."

"I'm paying for an awful lot since I lost my job."

"Pray that your book sells." She walked back to the front door. "Does your novel have a name?"

"*Virtual Velocity,*" he said with a nod.

She frowned. "What does that mean?" she asked after a pause.

"I can give you a definition," he said, "but it has nothing to do with the story."

"Wonderful. Perfect," she said with a nod.

He looked down and, staring at the floor, mumbled, "Do you think you could read it?" Glancing up at her, he added, "Probably had a better chance when I had the gun, right?"

The woman smiled and nodded. Jake was unsure whether she was agreeing with his last sentence, or agreeing to read his manuscript. She glanced back towards the bureau, walked over and, bending down, picked up a stray bullet on the floor. "A health hazard," she said, opening the bureau drawer and placing the bullet and the gun inside. "Someone could trip on it." She closed the drawer, walked back to the front door, opened it and motioned for Jake to exit.

"By the way," Jake asked as he walked past her, out the door, "what's your name?"

Becoming Jake
Summer 1966

I turned sixteen in 1966. A watershed year. The definitive year in rock & roll. If you don't believe me, check for yourself. It was also my definitive year. Probably not what you're thinking, that took two more years.

It was late August. A hot summer Los Angeles day. Even hot at the beach. No fog. No beach breeze. Glaring heat. It was one of those sun-in-full-throttle days. A perfect day. A day I had anticipated, hoped for, waited for. I put on swim trunks, a T-shirt, sneakers, midnight-dark wrap-around sunglasses and draped a beach towel around my neck. I stuffed my birthday money, which I had saved for this day, into my wallet, and with a confident air, headed down Wilshire Boulevard to Third Street. This was pre-Santa Monica Promenade monstrosity. It was to be my initial solo fashion purchase; my first self-bought shirt. From there I was off to go body surfing at Sorrento Beach. Like I said, a perfect day.

For those of you who haven't been there, Third Street is called Third Street, because it's three blocks from the Santa Monica beach. Clever. Back then, Third Street was a sleepy, quiet, drab stretch dotted with stores like Woolworth's, Newbury's and J.C. Penny. There was a small men's boutique clothing store about half a block south of Wilshire. I had never entered, but had stared through the window with the thought of one day not only striding inside as though I belonged, but making a definitive, confident purchase.

I arrived early and waited until 9 am for the doors to open. One door, singular, truth be told. Upon seeing me planted in the doorway, a tired-looking, portly, puffy, walrus-mustached man forced a smile. I readied myself, took a deep breath, and marched in. After he learned about my birthday haul and realized that I actually could make a purchase, his smile expanded into a full-blown used-car-salesman explosion. Motioning towards the back of the store, he led me to a sea-blue, long-sleeved western shirt with red and white horizontal stripes and white snap-on buttons. It was the coolest shirt I'd ever seen. The salesman agreed, grinning and nodding as he took my cash. He congratulated me on my taste, shook my hand and, placing a hand on my back, led me to the door. After less than ten minutes, I exited, wallet-emptied, carrying my shirt not in a bag, but proudly displayed on a hanger covered in see-through plastic. I draped it over my right shoulder, marching out in measured steps. It all looked very professional. I contemplated walking home and dropping off the shirt before heading to the beach. But I liked how people stared as I paraded past them and decided it would be safe wrapped as it was, as I body surfed.

I walked down Wilshire Boulevard, heading north on Palisades Park, down the ramp to the Pacific Coast Highway. Kids with transistors on high waited at the bottom of the ramp to cross with me. "Summer in the City," "96 Tears," and "Psychotic Reaction" came out of the small mono speakers before the light turned green. Walking through the beach parking lot that lead onto the sand, I took my time searching for a spot, the right spot, one neither too close nor too far from the water, laid my towel down and carefully draped my shirt so none of the plastic made contact with the sand. I then took off my shoes and shirt, hid my keys, sunglasses, and wallet under my towel and ran to the waves.

No matter how hot it is on the sand, the Pacific Ocean is always cold. It's best simply to brace yourself and dive in. It's not unlike a high-voltage electric shock, but it's short-lived and preferable to the slow incremental approach. The waves were good, between four and six feet and steady. I took waves, dove under them, and lost myself in the rush of the sea; the only form of baptism I've ever understood. A couple of hours later I came out wet, exhausted and happy. Carefully and meticulously positioning my shirt so it would be touched by neither sand nor my wet body, I laid back on the small strip of towel, slipped on my sunglasses, closed my eyes, and began planning the rest of the day. I'd lie down for a few minutes, to dry off.

I was never one to just lie on the beach; fifteen minutes was usually my limit, then I'd head home, stop at A&W Root Beer on Wilshire and 9th and grab lunch, maybe backtrack and stop at the record store and browse for a bit. But, I wasn't sure I wanted to drag my new shirt through all of Santa Monica. Probably just lunch and home to drop off my shirt, put on my sneakers and then head to the Lincoln gym. I'd meet Jim there at around three, we'd play pick-up basketball games for a couple of hours. The summer of '66 revolved around rock music, the beach, basketball, seeing films, and trying to figure out how to meet girls. The last was my weakest point. If we were feeling adventurous, and had extra cash, we might set out to Pacific Ocean Park, the amusement park that seemed to dangle over the ocean. But it seemed more like a movie night. It was between "How to Steal a Million," with Audrey Hepburn and Peter O'Toole, or "Modesty Blaise," starring Monica Vitti. I was a huge O'Toole fan, but Jim said the movie looked dumb and that Vitti was hot and there might be some topless scenes. Still, I figured, it was my night to choose and we could always see "Modesty Blaise" the next night. "Blow-Up" was something to consider, it was kind of like an art film. The trailer looked cool. David Hemmings plays a London photographer who spends his time photographing fashion models. That one actually could have nudity, plus I had read that there was a scene where the Yardbirds were playing, with both Jeff Beck and Jimmy Page. At the end, Beck slams his guitar against the amps, or the wall, or something like that. How cool is that? "Blow-Up" sounded like the coolest choice. But we were only prepared to go to films we could walk to, which meant the Arrow, the Criterion or the Wilshire, so at least for that night, "Blow-Up" was out of the picture. I was preparing my argument as to why "How to Steal a Million" was the film we were going to see when I heard: "Give me your shirt!" It was a girl's voice, simultaneously commanding and pleading.

I instinctively opened my eyes at the sound, but didn't look towards the voice, figuring whoever it was, was not talking to me.

"Your shirt. Now!" The voice was closer, louder, more insistent. "Quick! Give it to me!"

I looked up and saw an amazingly attractive, dark-haired, blue-eyed girl standing above me and glaring down. She was wearing bikini bottoms and... nothing else. A topless Aphrodite. A vision.

"The shirt!" she cried, looking back towards the parking lot. She bit her lower lip, a panicked expression on her face.

I sat up and stared, mute, unable to comprehend what I was seeing.

She impatiently bent down, grabbed my shirt, ripped off the plastic, unbuttoned it, pulled it off the hanger and hurriedly began to put it on. "I need to borrow this," she explained, again turning towards the parking lot.

"Yeah. Sure," I replied. Following her gaze, I could see a police car parked on the edge of the lot, its lights angrily flashing. A blue-suited officer was marching towards us.

"Should I run?" she asked, her breasts disappearing behind the fabric of my new shirt.

"He'll catch you," I said, looking back as he neared.

"Yeah. They already have Jenny. They'll find me anyway, right?"

"Right," I agreed. I stood and we both watched as he closed in.

"Shit!" she exclaimed. "This is going to ruin everything." She stared down at me, her eyes squinting, a questioning expression on her face. "I can trust you, right?"

I nodded exaggeratedly.

"You swear to God? I mean I can fucking, seriously trust you." It was more a statement, than a question.

Again I nodded.

"Give me your wallet. Hurry!"

I bent down, picked up my wallet and handed it to her.

"You see those towels?" She motioned towards two towels a few yards up the beach, as she opened my wallet and pulled out my driver's license. A license I had only owned for a month.

Another nod.

"That white bag sitting on the blue towel is mine. My wallet and my keys are in it." Sliding my license in my shirt pocket, she tossed my wallet on the beach towel, grabbed my arm and pulled me towards her. "Listen to what I'm telling you."

"I am," I said, hoping she'd keep me in her grasp.

Releasing her grip, she continued buttoning my shirt. Her breasts pushing against the fabric. "Maybe nothing will happen, maybe he'll let me go, but, just in case..." she paused, looked back and, seeing how quickly he was gaining ground, began speaking at rapid-fire speed, "I'll give you back your license once this is all over. Insurance," she added. "I live at 1502 Euclid, a few blocks north of Wilshire. The apartment is 205. I drive a green 1965 Mustang that's parked on the west side of the lot in the first row. It has a UCLA bumper sticker. The keys are in my purse. Grab my purse, find my car and drive to my apartment." Again she grabbed my arm and shook it. "Are you listening?" she cried.

I nodded mutely. We both watched as the grimacing officer sloughed through the sand.

"As you enter the apartment, my bedroom is the one to the right," she said, speaking quickly and authoritatively. "My nightstand has two drawers. The bottom drawer is locked. There's a key on my keychain that will open it. Unlock that drawer and underneath some papers and envelopes, you'll find an envelope with money. I might need bail and I don't want to call my father. He cannot know about this. He will kill me. Literally! Grab the envelope and drive down to the Santa Monica Police station. That's probably where they're going to take me. I'll pay you for this, but don't fuck me over. I have your license. I know where you..."

The officer cut her short, stopping abruptly in front of us and silently glowering down at my shirt. He was a big, tall, brawny blonde, looking to be in his late twenties. "What the hell do you think you're doing?" he snapped, a practiced officious scowl on his face. "We're going to the station," he declared before she could reply.

"But I'm not doing anything, officer," she protested.

"They all saw it," he said, motioning towards the crowd standing by the police car. "We've had several complaints and people willing to make complaints in writing. So we're going." He turned to me, his eyes narrow and squinty. "Who are you?" he demanded.

"He's my boyfriend," she replied defiantly.

The officer looked at me with an incredulous expression. "Yeah?" he asked, staring at me with a disdainful frown. "Doing strip shows on the beach and robbing the cradle."

"He's mature for his age," she replied with a composed smile. "Where are you taking me? Where should I have him pick me up?"

"Santa Monica jail," he said, "and we're going now." He moved to grab her arm, but rethinking it, pointed towards the patrol car. "And I don't know when you're going to be able to go anywhere." She shrugged, buttoned the last button of my shirt and headed towards the parking lot.

As I walked behind them, she turned, smiled at me and winked. I smiled back, but she had already looked away. A crowd was growing, following us to the police car like some ragged beach parade. People were laughing, fingers pointing, guys yelling for her to take it off. I wanted to sock them.

Personally, I was beaming. She had introduced me as her boyfriend. She could just as easily have introduced me as her friend, cousin, or brother, but she chose boyfriend. I smiled proudly as I marched in procession towards the waiting patrol car. Once there, I saw her friend sitting in the back seat, head hung down dejectedly. We stopped in front of the police car and a second officer walked over. "Turn around," he barked, looking her up and down. She shrugged and did as he commanded. They had her face the car and put her hands behind her back. I then watched as the first officer took out a set of handcuffs.

"You don't need to do that," I said, as they clamped the handcuffs on.

The officers stopped, turned towards me and glared. "What?" they snapped in unison.

In a low shaky voice, I started to repeat, "You don't..."

"Shut the fuck up," the blonde hulk directed, "or you're coming as well. We'll book you for obstruction."

"Go," she commanded, looking at me with a frown. "1502 #205. Go!"

"Right," I said, trying to exude a sense of confidence. "I'll see you... there."

The officer moved her to the side of the patrol car, opened the back door and, pushing her head down, guided her into the back seat.

"Right," I repeated to myself. I ran to where her towels were, grabbed her purse, opened it and found her wallet and her keys. The first thing I did was check her license. Her name was Kathrine Dawson. She was nineteen, going on twenty—almost four years older than I was—and still she had introduced me as her boyfriend. That continued to resonate. I picked up her bag, slid her wallet back in her purse, and, carrying her keys in my hand, raced back towards the beach parking lot in search of a green 1965 Mustang with a UCLA bumper sticker.

I found it within the first couple of minutes, put the key in the lock, and the door miraculously opened. Looking in, my sense of relief came to an abrupt halt. She drove a stick shift—I didn't. I'd practiced with my dad. We had tried a stick once in an empty parking lot. It was not pretty. My dad drove me home in silence and never suggested that we try it again. Not the most pleasant of memories, but I thought I remembered the basics. The scariest part was going to be driving up the ramp from the Pacific Coast Highway on to Ocean Boulevard. If I made it that far, I was sure I could manage the rest. Remembering the vision of Kathrine, I figured I could do whatever was needed. Standing by the Mustang, I searched the parking lot until I saw a shirtless guy, hands in his jean pockets, swaggering my way. He seemed to be in his mid-twenties, had long sand-colored hair—one of those guys who rebuilds transmissions, can fix whatever breaks—one of those. I figured if he could do all that, he'd know how to drive a stick. I embarrassedly called out to him, explained that the Mustang was my sister's car. It hurt to say sister instead of girlfriend, but, anyway, I explained that it was her car, she had gotten very ill, probably food poisoning (I was going for realism), had been taken to the hospital in an ambulance, and I had to get her car home. She had just purchased the car, or so my story went. I'd never driven it and I had never driven a stick. I felt myself cringe as I asked if he could show me the basics. I quickly checked in Kathrine's wallet and saw she had thirty dollars. I offered him ten for the lesson. The guy looked at me quizzically. He then smiled, shrugged and said "Why not?"

I spent the next fifteen minutes taking what was a near crash course in driving a stick. After many jeers and honks and close-to-panicked yells, he said. "Okay bro, you're on your own." I think he said "bro." Did we say "bro" in the sixties? I don't remember.

Anyway, he left and it was me and the Mustang. I got in, started the ignition, and put the car in reverse. Only then did it hit me I had no driver's license, or more accurately, the license I had was Kathrine's. Odds were good that as I lunged and gasped towards her apartment I'd be pulled over and if so, I'd probably be taking a similar trip in a patrol car. With that thought, I began the slow crawl from the Sorrento Beach parking lot to 1502 Euclid. The drive itself was no more than fifteen minutes in duration—a short block down Pacific Coast Highway, then left and up the ramp, right on Ocean and left on Wilshire Boulevard to 15th—but it was a symphony of gear grinding, heart pounding, and cars honking.

Hands strangling the steering wheel, I turned left on 15th, parked in front of her apartment, placed my forehead on the wheel and took perhaps my first breath since exiting the parking lot. Hers was a typical Santa Monica street. Well-manicured, dotted with long-necked palm trees that ended in static explosions of fronds. North of Wilshire. More on the upscale part of the city. I exited, locked the car door and, with her purse lodged safely under my arm and her keys in hand, dashed towards apartment #205. Taking two steps at a time, I hurried up the concrete stairs, past two doors until I stood directly in front of her apartment. I came to a dead stop and stared at the door, unsure of what to do next. Even with her permission, I felt like an intruder. My hand was shaking as I guided the key towards the lock.

The door opened. I cautiously entered, expecting at any second for someone to rush out of one of the bedrooms, gun-in-hand, and finding an intruder—fire. I closed the door behind me and stood motionless. There was a TV, a worn green sofa, and two brown bean bag chairs. Towards the back there was a small dining table with two chairs. Warhol and Dali prints hung on the walls, along with posters of the Beatles and Elvis. I took a deep breath, and, following her directions, turned right and headed towards her bedroom.

I came to the entrance and stopped. I closed my eyes, then opening them again, I breathed in deeply, leaned in and surveyed the room. There was a set of drawers, a double bed which was partially made, and a bedside table on which sat a medium-sized lamp, with an overly-frilly pink lampshade. A tri-fold mirror vanity with two storage cases, three drawers and a dressing stool was placed against the wall by the door. On the other side of the room was a leather chair that was overflowing with books, albums, and clothes. On the top she had slung a bra and a pair of panties. I remained planted, mouth ajar, cemented in the doorway. I placed my hands between the door jams to keep myself steady and upright. Slowly, on tiptoes, I entered. A little over an hour before, I had seen naked breasts for the first time, her breasts, and now here I was, alone in her bedroom. I could see and touch whatever I wanted. She was most likely locked in a jail cell anxiously waiting for me to arrive, cash in hand. But, like a voyager landing on a new world, I moved slowly.

I walked towards the middle of the room. There I centered myself, took two deep breaths and again closed my eyes. I counted to ten, opened my eyes and walked, clockwise, around her bedroom, taking in every piece of furniture, every article of clothing, every photo, painting, book, knickknack—every item. On the ledge of a south-facing window sat three cactus plants in tiny pots. Underneath the window, was an RCA Victor record player with speakers. It was blue. Looked like a girl's record player. To the side of it was a row of albums held between two rust-colored bricks. I moved towards them and crouching down, studied her collection. There was "I Hear a Symphony" by the Supremes, "Strangers in the Night" by Frank Sinatra, "I Couldn't Live Without Your Love" by Petula Clark and "Je m'appelle Barbra" by Barbara Streisand. There were also singles, "You Don't Have to Say You Love Me" by Dusty Springfield, "Hungry" by Paul Revere and the Raiders, "Paperback Writer" by the Beatles. Pretty disappointing stuff. No Stones, Them, Kinks, Byrds, Buffalo Springfield, Cream, or Yardbirds. I found that a bit depressing.

At sixteen, I prided myself on my exquisite musical sensibilities and wanted her tastes to reflect my exacting standards. I walked over to the player and saw that on the turntable was a copy of Love's first album. I carefully picked it up and stared at it. I almost felt that I needed to sit down. I didn't know any girls who liked Love. To be honest I didn't know that many girls back then, but still. Later Love would release "Forever Changes," one of the best rock albums of all time. One of the only albums that could rival "Pet Sounds," which came out in, yes, 1966. So even though she had Sinatra, Streisand and that stuff, she had Love. How cool was that? I was tempted to play the album and give myself a soundtrack I could remember. But it would have been too uncomfortable, I needed to be able to hear any unexpected sounds. I put the album back on the turntable and continued my exploration.

Next to the albums was a bookshelf that stood about four feet high. Above the bookshelf she had hung a poster of the TAMI show, along with a ticket stub, that she'd glued to the bottom. Black and white photos ran along the top and the sides like a semi frame, along with the names of the acts who had performed: The Barbarians, The Beach Boys, Chuck Berry, James Brown and The Famous Flames, Marvin Gaye (with backing vocals by The Blossoms), Gerry & the Pacemakers, Lesley Gore, Jan and Dean, Billy J. Kramer and The Dakotas, Smokey Robinson and The Miracles, the Supremes, and The Rolling Stones. People talk about Woodstock, Coachella, Isle of White, but it was the TAMI show that changed the course of rock history. My sister went, but I didn't. It is one of those lifetime regrets.

Beneath the poster, on top of the bookshelf, stood four photos encased in gold and silver-colored frames with those little stands that kick out in the back to hold them up. One displayed a picture of Kathrine at her graduation. Dressed in grey cap and gown, she stood alone, erect, at attention, eyes bright, beaming at the camera. In another she was wearing a yellow summer dress, smiling, more at-ease, relaxed, flashing a bright high-beam smile. Standing next to her was, I suppose, her perfectly-normal-looking mother and father. To the right of them stood an oafish, smirking, belligerent-looking younger brother. Next was a photo of her in a tight-fitting, emerald-green evening dress. At her side, with his arm offensively curving round her back, stood a tall, suit-wearing jock type. They were probably seniors then and he was most likely captain of the football team. Practiced at bullying freshmen, shoving them to the floor then grabbing them by the ankles and hanging them upside-down out the school second-story window. It was an unsettling photo to look at. The fourth photo was a black and white shot of her as a young girl, dressed in jean shorts and a T-shirt, down on one knee, grinning as she proudly hugged her German Shepherd. I liked that one.

Scanning down, the second shelf was filled with books, titles I didn't know, by authors I'd mostly never heard of. I quickly looked them over and then starting at the beginning slowly scanned each one. I searched until I found a notebook and pen beside her bedside bureau. Then, walking back to the bookshelf, I crouched down, pulled a sheet out of the notebook and began to write down the names as I said them aloud. Apart from James Joyce and F. Scott Fitzgerald, the names were foreign to me—Tropic of Cancer by Henry Miller, The Diary of Anaïs Nin, Lonesome Traveler by Jack Kerouac, The Immoralist by Andre Gide, To the Lighthouse by Virginia Woolf, The Stranger by Albert Camus, and Valley of the Dolls by Jacqueline Suzanne. I now see what an outlier Suzanne was but had no idea at the time. I wrote down all of the names and book titles, folded the sheet and shoved it into my shirt pocket.

I returned the notebook to the bottom shelf which held books on literature and theory as well as other notebooks crammed with class notes, drawings, and doodles. I fingered through the notebooks, studying her handwriting, captivated by the way she formed a "y" or an "s." I was unsure what to make of the fact that she surrounded herself with books and literature.

I searched, hoping to find a diary, personal writings, revelations. But I knew I should have been on my way to the Santa Monica jail by then. Standing, I gave her photos a final look, turned and walked to the dresser drawers directly opposite the bed. There I stopped, took in two deep breaths and began. Crouching down, I started with the bottom drawer, methodically working my way up. The bottom two drawers housed sweaters, T-shirts, shorts, scarfs, socks, pajamas and the like. I carefully studied them, imaging her in them; amazed at how small the waists were. I examined the various articles, then placed them back, trying to make it look as though they had not been touched or disturbed. Moving up to the top drawer, I again stopped and breathed in deeply. I slid it open and stared down at a drawer filled with bras and panties. I stood perfectly still, peering down as one does at a deep-sea aquarium, staring into a hidden, previously unseen world. I reached in, picked up one of her bras and rubbed my hand against the smooth inside. The cups were soft against my fingers. I placed it back in the drawer and for a long while, stared at a wisp of light egg-blue cloth. Picking it up, I gingerly held up the panties, studying them as one would a found treasure. I then abruptly stopped, remembered my charge, and placed them back exactly as I'd found them. I was tempted to take one. I again picked the blue pair, reconsidered, put them back and slid the drawer shut. I wanted to stay, explore, but she was waiting for me, locked in a jail cell, covered in little more than my new shirt. It was my responsibility to find the money, hurry back. She was now my obligation. Still, the magnetic pull was strong.

I shut the drawer, made my way to her bedside bureau and following her instructions, guided a key towards the keyhole in the bureau. Miraculously, the first key I tried worked, the drawer unlocked and slid open. It was one of those deep-bottom drawers filled with folders, envelopes, and papers. On the top was her passport. She'd been to London, Paris, Rome, Madrid, Montreux, and Mexico City. I'd been nowhere. I stared at her passport photo. She was smiling directly at me. I felt a jolt, a deep lonely yearning. I closed the passport, placed it back in the drawer and picking up certificates, quickly thumbed through them. Her diploma from Santa Monica High School was there along with a certificate that seemed to be from a UCLA sorority—my girlfriend was a UCLA sorority member. I put them back, dug further down, and came across a sealed manila envelope and opened it. Inside were hundred-dollar bills. All told there were fifty hundred-dollar bills, five thousand dollars in hundred-dollar bills. I had never seen, much less held that much money. I placed the bills on the bed and spread them out. I then leaped onto the bed landing on top of them, as though swimming in cash. I'm not quite sure why I did that, but leap I did. I then gathered myself and carefully collecting the bills, slid them back in the envelope and placed it on the bed. I pulled out the passport, took one long final look at the photo. As I replaced the passport, I saw a small photo album wedged at the bottom of the drawer. Picking it up, I sat back down on the bed and carefully turning the pages, studied the photos. There were only a few. One of her at her graduation, sticking out her tongue at the camera, another of her in some foreign city wearing jeans, aqua-colored blouse, her hair in a ponytail. There were four of her at the beach in the now infamous blue bikini. In two she was with her friend who was now in jail with her. They grinned as they pretended to slug one another. In another she was striking a severe mock-modeling pose. I stared at the photos as if trying to memorize them, mentally scan them, imprint them in my brain. This was before smart phones, before any image could be duplicated, carried in your pocket and saved forever, before any and all images were ubiquitous and therefore commonplace.

As I was placing the album back, I noticed a small manila envelope at the bottom of the drawer. I placed the album on the bed, picked up the envelope and opening it poured the contents onto the bed. Five polaroid photos fell out. In them Kathrine was as she was when I first saw her. She was on the beach, smiling at the camera wearing only her blue bikini bottoms. In one she was standing hands on hips, another hands locked over her head, a third pointing her fingers at the camera as though they were guns. In the fourth she was standing up looking away, apparently unaware that the photo was being taken.

She looked pensive, as if searching for something. There was no overt grinning or posing for the camera. It was simply her looking at or for something and in the fifth, she stood totally naked, her back to the camera, looking back, a slight smile on her face. I picked each one up, found treasure, and studied it. Placing one down, I'd pick up the next and then repeat the process.

The phone by her bedside blasted a loud, shrill ring. I jumped and dropped the photo as though I'd been apprehended by the sound. I stared at the white princess phone as it rang insistently, convinced that whoever was on the other line knew where I was and what I was doing. Finally, it was silent again. I waited on edge, prepared for the ringing to start up again. It didn't. I glanced at the small white clock on her bed stand and realized I had to go. I slid the photos back in the envelope, placed it precisely where I had found it in the drawer, put the photo album and other envelopes on top of it, locked it and headed towards the door. I stopped, did an about face, ran back to the bureau, unlocked the drawer, quickly took everything out, removed the photos out of the small manila envelope, slid the one of Kathrine looking away from the camera into my T-shirt pocket, placed everything back in the drawer, and locked it.

Staring at the photo, I sat there contemplating my next move. I thought I heard the front door open. I was sure it hadn't, but what if it had. I leaped off the bed, slid the photo back in my pocket, quickly put her panties back in the top drawer and raced out of the bedroom.

The apartment was empty, silent. I took one final look around her living room and opened the front door. I paused and stared down the hall to her bedroom. I then exited, closing the front door so as not to make a sound and, as silently as possible, walked down the apartment stairs to her Mustang.

I tossed her purse and the cash-filled envelope on the passenger's seat, started the car, made a U-turn back towards Wilshire and pressed down on the accelerator. I was getting the hang of the stick shift and felt a rush as I replayed all that had happened since I'd bought my shirt. I dialed up the radio, and sang aloud to "Wild Thing" as I headed towards the police station to bail my girlfriend out of jail.

Arriving at the Santa Monica Courthouse, I parked in the lot by the Santa Monica Civic Auditorium, where the one and only annual TAMI Show had been held. It was still an active venue in those days. I had seen the Yardbirds there, but not with Jeff Beck. Grabbing the envelope and her purse out of the back seat, I hurried out of the car and ran to the City Hall building, unsure how I was going to figure out where she was being held. As I entered the building and looked for an information desk, I heard a female voice call out, "Hey!"

I turned and there she was, sitting on a long wooden bench that was placed against the wall, wrapped in my magical shirt. I stopped, smiled and headed towards her. I felt like a thief. I was a thief. I had never stolen anything before, but there lay the proof of my larceny in my shirt pocket. As I neared her, I was filled with the realization that I had entered her world unexpectedly. There had been no preparation. Nothing had been tidied, sanitized, hidden or arranged. I knew her and was overwhelmed by that knowledge. She stood and walked towards me, I placed my hand in my pocket, checking that the photo was secure. Convinced that it could be seen. "You're out?" I said.

"Was never in," she replied with a shake of her head. "They just wanted to scare us. Wanted to teach us a lesson, they said. "Where were you?" she asked. "What took so long? I tried calling, but you didn't pick up."

I just nodded, not knowing how to respond.

She shrugged and continued. "That jerk cop who arrested me asked for my number. He said we could start off ahead of the game, since he'd already handcuffed me." She paused, as though awaiting a response, but I stood, staring at her in silence, not thinking of anything to say. "So," she continued, "I told him I couldn't go out with him because I had a boyfriend."

Again I nodded stupidly, too afraid to ask if she meant me.

She looked down at the envelope and purse in my hand. "Thanks," she said, reaching over and taking them from me. "So I could trust you."

I smiled and looked away.

"I thought so. Guess I get to keep my millions. And you look good with a purse," she added. "The color suits you."

I grinned and nodded. "Where's your friend?" I asked.

"Her boyfriend drove down and picked her up. It was a while ago. I'm surprised you didn't run into them at the apartment. What took you so long anyway?"

I cringed at the thought that her roommate and boyfriend could have walked in on me mid-reverie. "I haven't driven a stick in a while," I explained. "Took me a bit to get used to it again."

She stared at me and cocked her head. She then laughed. "Hope my gears aren't ground to death. You park out in the lot?" she asked, motioning me to follow as she walked towards the front door.

"Out by the Civic," I said.

"I'll drive you home," she replied, motioning for me to follow. "Least I can do. And I need to get your shirt back to you. Can't very well take it off and give it to you here."

I felt myself blush. "Looks better on you," I said. She smiled, which melted me. "I left my stuff at the beach," I added, motioning towards the ocean. "I'd better go back and get it."

"I'll drive you. Come on."

"That's okay," I said. "I'll walk. It's close. I can use the exercise."

"You sure?" she asked. "No problem. Like I said, I owe you."

"I noticed your books," I said nervously looking away. "On your bookshelf. You have some cool books."

"You into books?"

I shrugged. "I like Salinger," I said. "Steinbeck."

"They're cool." She nodded. "I'm a Lit major. I want to write," she added with an embarrassed smile.

"Books?" I asked stupidly.

"That's the plan, which in the real world, as my parents constantly explain, means I'm going to end up teaching." She paused, bit her bottom lip and shook her head as if dismissing her last sentence. "Most of those books are for school. I mean Camus, Gide, Sartre... they're assigned. They're cool, but to be honest, not stuff I'd generally be reading. I like some Fitzgerald. I'm a Woolf fan; Miller." She paused and stared as though she was silently asking me a question. "You read Henry Miller? Kerouac?"

I shook my head, embarrassed I wasn't familiar with the names.

"You should." Again she took a slight pause. "You write?"

'Yeah," I said, automatically. "I write." I didn't.

She nodded. "Yeah. What?"

"Stuff," I replied with a shrug.

"Cool." She stared at me as though she was about to speak, but simply smiled. Her eyes shifted from green to blue with the light. "How about I cook you dinner next week to thank you?"

"Don't need to thank me," I said, looking away and trying to keep my voice from rising.

"Sure I do. Sir Galahad. You went above and beyond. How about next Tuesday? What do you like to eat?"

"Anything," I said with an embarrassed shrug.

She opened her purse and took out a pen, "Hold out your hand," she commanded.

I did so and, taking my hand in hers, she wrote her name and phone number. Working her way up my arm, she wrote the names Jack Kerouac, Henry Miller, Anais Nin, and Virginia Woolf. "There, you're tattooed," she said with a smile. "You have your homework assignment." Tapping at her phone number, she added, "Call me and we can confirm the time."

I smiled and nodded.

"I better go hide my cash. Thanks," she said smiling broadly and hugging me. It happened so quickly I wasn't able to take it in. It was over before I knew it had happened, which is something that I've always regretted. Life does that. You're not prepared and it swoops in and it's gone before you've even noticed. "I'll return your shirt, when you come over, okay?" She smiled, turned and walked towards her car. "Your license," she said, stopping turning back. Reaching into my new shirt, she pulled out my license and stared at it. "You take a good picture, John Jensen." She held it out.

"Thanks," I said, taking the license and sliding it into my pocket, next to her picture.

"I like Jake better than John," she said. "I've always wanted to know a Jake. I'll call you Jake."

I smiled and nodded.

"Okay Jake, then I'll see you on Tuesday. Call me."

"Cool" I replied with a nod.

I never did. I figured there was no upside to it. I was already lost, head over heels, had fallen down twenty rabbit holes. She was gorgeous, I'd entered her secret world, seen her photos, her books, her breasts, her world. If I'd gone, I would have been gawky, tongue-tied, terrified. She would have done her best to entertain me and fulfill her obligation. She would have done her good deed and gone on with her life and I would have left as strung out as any junkie.

Or, for argument's sake, let's say she found an awkward sixteen-year-old kid attractive, or liked to deflower teenage boys, or was willing to show her thanks and appreciation to the fullest extent. What if she had been my first? What if that night I exited that room fully transformed? A dream come true? The start of a new life?

A disaster. A total disaster. As soon as I walked out the door, she would have returned to her life filled with classes, books, college friends and boyfriends. I would have been left spinning at the edge of the universe. Even at sixteen, I knew myself well enough to know nothing good would have come of that. That one night wouldn't have been worth losing everything I'd gained. Best keep my memories intact and escape with some semblance of sanity. Or, maybe it wasn't that at all. Maybe I was just a sixteen-year-old who had yet to kiss a girl, and was just too scared to show up.

Plus, and this is a huge plus, I had the photo. She'd eventually know it was gone. She'd know who had taken it. How would I explain that? She said she knew she could trust me. I hoped she'd remember that. She could. The photo was just for me. Not to be shared. Not even Jim would see that photo.

As I walked, towards the beach, I put my hand in my pocket and touched it. A talisman. I don't remember the walk, too many feelings and thoughts short-circuiting my nervous system. When I got to the shore, I took the piece of paper with the list of writers out of my pocket and, along with her photo and my license, carefully placed them together, and removing my T-shirt, folded and covered them with my beach towel. I then headed to the shore to go body surfing again. After a few steps, I stopped, turned around and walked back. I couldn't leave the photo there unprotected. I put on my T-shirt, securely placed my license and her photo in my pocket, draped my towel over my shoulders and headed back. Walking up Wilshire towards home, I stopped at A&W Root Beer on 9th and bought a coke and an order of fries. I was suddenly ravenous. I'd missed lunch, but hadn't felt it until then. I then headed home. Luckily no one was there. I didn't want to talk to anyone. I went into my room, shut the door, took out the photo and stared at it. I stared for a long time. I placed it along with the list of authors in my secret drawer. I then went to the bathroom and took a shower. Her number and the writers' names were erased by the soap and water. She was gone.

For months I fantasized going back, showing up, flowers in hand. But I never went. From that day on I insisted on being called Jake, a move my family and friends initially rejected, but I held firm. I followed the list I had scribbled on the piece of paper while kneeling in front of her bookcase. For the next several months, I made regular pilgrimages to the library and buried myself in the writers on the list. I then wrote my first short story. It was called "Kathrine." That's all I remember about it, which is probably for the best. She had led me to a new world, reset my life course, named me. Without Kathrine, there would have been no Jake.

The End

Note from the Author

Word-of-mouth is crucial for any author to succeed. If you enjoyed
the book, please leave a review online—anywhere you are able. Even
if it's just a sentence or two. It would make all the difference and
would be very much appreciated.

Thanks!
Anthony

About the Author

Anthony Mora's works have been compared to Fante, Pinter and Salinger. A novelist and a playwright, his first novel was *BANG! A Love Story*. Linda Cardellini starred in the original play adaptation of "BANG!" In Los Angeles and New York. Anthony served as the playwright-in-residence at The Sidewalk Studio Theatre. He has had seven plays produced including "POP," "Modern Love," and "Silencing Silas." *Virtual Velocity* is his second novel.

Photo taken by Jeanna Sabatino

Thank you so much for reading one of our **Literary Fiction** novels.

If you enjoyed our book, please check out our recommended title for your next great read!

The Five Wishes by Mr. Murray McBride by Joe Siple

2018 Maxy Award "Book of the Year"
2018 PenCraft Award 1st Place "Fiction-Drama"
2018 American Fiction Awards Finalist
2018 ScreenCraft Cinematic Book Award Finalist
2018 Wishing Shelf Award (UK) Finalist

"A sweet...tale of human connection...will feel familiar to fans of Hallmark movies." *–KIRKUS REVIEWS*

"An emotional story that will leave readers meditating on the life-saving magic of kindness." *–Indie Reader*

View other Black Rose Writing titles at
www.blackrosewriting.com/books and use promo code

PRINT to receive a **20% discount** when purchasing.